D0311041

R IS FOR **REBEL**

J. ANDERSON COATS

R is for REBEL

Atheneum
Atheneum Books for Young Readers
NEW YORK LONDON TORONTO SYDNEY NEW DELHI

A
atheneum

ATHENEUM BOOKS FOR YOUNG READERS

An imprint of Simon & Schuster Children's Publishing Division

1230 Avenue of the Americas, New York, New York 10020

This book is a work of fiction. Any references to historical events, real people, or real places are used fictitiously. Other names, characters, places, and events are products of the author's imagination, and any resemblance to actual events or places or persons, living or dead, is entirely coincidental.

Text copyright © 2018 by J. Anderson Coats

Cover illustration copyright © 2018 by Maike Plenzke

All rights reserved, including the right of reproduction in whole or in part in any form.

ATHENEUM BOOKS FOR YOUNG READERS is a registered trademark of Simon & Schuster, Inc. Atheneum logo is a trademark of Simon & Schuster, Inc.

For information about special discounts for bulk purchases, please contact Simon & Schuster Special Sales at 1-866-506-1949 or business@simonandschuster.com.

The Simon & Schuster Speakers Bureau can bring authors to your live event. For more information or to book an event, contact the Simon & Schuster Speakers Bureau at 1-866-248-3049 or visit our website at www.simonspeakers.com.

Also available in an Atheneum Books for Young Readers hardcover edition

Interior design by Brad Mead

The text for this book was set in Italian Old Style MT.

Manufactured in the United States of America

0119 OFF

First Atheneum Books for Young Readers paperback edition February 2019

10 9 8 7 6 5 4 3 2 1

The Library of Congress has cataloged the hardcover edition as follows:

Names: Coats, J. Anderson (Jillian Anderson), author.

Title: R is for rebel / J. Anderson Coats.

Description: First edition. | New York : Atheneum Books for Young Readers, [2018]

Summary: After her parents are jailed for a failed resistance movement, Malley is sent to reform school, where she plans some resistance of her own.

Identifiers: LCCN 2017007502 | ISBN 9781481496674 (hardcover) | ISBN 9781481496681 (pbk) | ISBN 9781481496698 (eBook)

Subjects: | CYAC: Conduct of life—Fiction. | Reformatories—Fiction. | Schools—Fiction. | Government, Resistance to—Fiction. | Nuns—Fiction.

Classification: LCC PZ7.1.C62 Raai 2018 | DDC [Fic]—dc23

LC record available at https://lccn.loc.gov/2017007502

To my grands

Sylvia
Sody
Mary Lou
Hilding

In memoriam

DAY 1

DAY 1

IT TAKES HALF THE CONSTABULARY TO BRING me in to national school.

I lead them a merry chase, though.

Over croplands new-sown with barley and through a gap in the hedge that puts me in a sprawling, manicured pasture—they expect me to head for the greenwood, ha!—past the hanging tree with its lingering noose and toward the broad, rushing river. I'm halfway across the covered bridge when two of the big oafs appear at the other end, hulking against the flat gray sky beyond.

There's no question of going back the way I came. There's only one other choice, but it's a good ten feet of drop, that current looks treacherous, and I can't swim.

Captain Lennart pulls me off the guardrail as I'm about to jump into the surging black water below.

I want to say I see a ripple of sympathy cross Captain Lennart's face as he's marching me toward the school's detention wagon. He's the one who argued for clemency when my parents were convicted of treason, who insisted that the only decent thing to do was transport me to the penal colony with them.

But the judge took one look at me, trussed up like I was in that silly pink dress the lawyer made me wear, and announced it would be cruel to sentence me to my parents' fate when I was still a child with a moldable mind, and a victim of their disgraceful influence as well. The whole point of the Education Act was to give Milean kids a proper chance in life by sending us to national school so we'd learn the deference and compliance and proper work ethic that would ensure our successful future in the Wealdan empire—things we'd never learn in our ignorant, superstitious households. My parents were already in violation of the act, and it was the Crown's solemn duty to take me in hand and preserve my future from any further damage. *That*, said the judge, was the only decent thing to do.

Captain Lennart marches me up the wagon steps. His grip is secure but not painful, and I don't bother trying to break away. Not with a dozen constables around and not without a head start. Once I'm in, Captain Lennart swings the door behind me and bolts it shut. It's musty but dry inside, not nearly the stinking, jam-packed crates from the Burning Days when Milea first fell. I must know a thousand songs about how the grandmas and granddas were hauled off to the workhouses where they labored till they died, carving out roads and mining coal to pay back the Crown for the cost of the invasion and seizure of their homeland.

This wagon has two small barred windows, one on either side. Now that I'm catching my breath, it's starting to sink in. All of it. Those days on the run. Sleeping rough. Eating rougher. How far away my parents are already. How I'm ending up in the very place they fought so hard to keep me out of, where I won't know a soul. My eyes start to sting, so I put my face up to one of the windows and sing "The Noble-Hearted Three" as loud as I can. I'm just at the part where the heroic rebels are hacking the locks off a prison wagon very much like this one to free their comrades bound for the gallows when a constable drums his fist on the outside of the wagon, right by my ear.

"Shut it!" he shouts. "Or it'll be lashes for singing out-lawed songs!"

I bite my lip, hard, because twenty strokes with a whip marks you in more ways than one, and most of these constables are using their service to fulfill the Crown's military entrance requirements so they can train to become one of the graycoated butchers that pass for soldiers. I retreat a few paces while muttering swears in Milean, but real quiet so the big ox can't threaten me with lashes for speaking an outlawed tongue as well.

The constables are laughing now, wondering what kind of medals the Crown will pin on them for chasing down and bringing in the only child of the murderous, machine-breaking arsonists who were recently transported to the empire's most notorious penal colony for the rest of their natural lives. Those brutes are talking loud so I'll be sure to hear.

Well, they can send me to national school. Whether they can keep me quiet is another matter.

DAY 2

I HAVE TO PEE. I HOLD IT AS LONG AS I CAN before banging on the front wall to ask for a privy stop. There's a murmur of chatter, then a harsh laugh, but soon the wagon lurches to a halt. The back door swings open and I'm given a chance to get down and *do my business.*

"Unsupervised," the constable says, "but don't make me regret that mercy."

I nod, looking him in the feet like I've been taught, and duck behind a hedge. The crisp, woody smell, the damp ground underfoot—all at once I'm back home, sitting for secret lessons taught entirely in Milean by a raggedy scarecrow of a man we called Master Grenallan, though even the tiniest kids knew that wasn't his real name. Hedge school was about the only thing that could lure me away from our homestead and its greening croplands and excellent climbing trees and long, dusty deer paths crowded with berry bushes humming with a million-million bees. I never missed a lesson once I learned I was breaking at least three Wealdan laws each time I went.

Milea fell but three generations before I was born, quickly and decisively, and each time I do something Milean—even small things—I feel a subtle wash of warmth, like my ancestors are placing gentle hands on my head in a blessing. Like they're comforted to know that their despairing, doomed defense of our land hasn't been forgotten. Their songworthy acts taught me everything I know about resisting. Survival, too. Where I'm going, the tighter I hold on to the past, the more likely I'll stay someone my ancestors and my parents can be proud of. The more likely I'll stay Milean, no matter how hard the Wealdans try to make me forget.

Later, when the sun is slanting lower through the window bars and lighting up the inside of the wagon a golden tawny color, a big whiff of new-turned earth brings me to the nearest window. Sure enough, we're rolling past a length of cropland, where Mileans are running narrow plows up the furrows while folds of dirt spill out behind them. If I didn't know better, I'd say they were cheerful and content and industrious, especially considering there are few things more glorious than running a plow on a bright spring day with the breeze at your back and the sun on your topknot.

I do know better, though. Those men and women are tenants on land that once was theirs, and now they must work it for Wealdan landlords.

There are also no kids clod-busting or weeding or playing alongside them. No one over three and under seventeen. Not since the Education Act emptied homesteads and villages of children, one by one.

DAY 5

MY SHOULDERS AND LEGS ARE THROBBING when the wagon heaves to yet another stop. The back door swings open to reveal a tidy green lawn and the slanting shadow of a huge square building. In the distance there's a low bank of hills, and none of it looks familiar. Not even a little.

I'm nowhere near Trelawney Crossing anymore.

"We're here." The bigger constable blocks my view. "You gonna climb down?"

I look him in the feet. I grip my shirttail so my hands won't tremble. Being manhandled out of the wagon by aspiring graycoats is going to end in bruises and sore ribs and crushed toes, but my first act here will *not* be one of compliance. When I give no response at all, the constables haul me out and march me up a broad pebbled path.

I've known for months this moment would come. My parents never kept any of their plans from me, and they couldn't dodge the constabulary forever. My da with his big farmer's hands and my ma all curves spilling everywhere, with forty ribbons in her topknot. They would not want me to cry. Not for them. Not for what they did. If my parents were here now, they'd start humming outlawed songs about Mileans whose sacrifices were greater than theirs—one-handed Everard forced to watch his children hang, Jasperine with her rifle and a price on her head—and soon I'd be humming along. I wouldn't be thinking how I should be reroofing the chicken run on our homestead on a brilliant sunny day or filling pail after pail with cider apples as the season turned. I wouldn't keep expecting to hear Master Grenallan's bird-whistle call that drew us behind the hedges for lessons out of sight of Wealdan inquisitors.

So I won't cry for what my parents did, but I can't promise I won't ever cry for them.

Forswelt National School is big and brick and sprawling, hemmed in by a tall bristle of iron fence, but it's well kept and even has the look of a factory. Nothing like the bleak, squalid workhouses that chewed up the grands during the Burning Days and now do the same to criminals regardless of their birth. The door I'm being marched toward is twice my height, made of sturdy weathered planks crosshatched with thick metal. The constables bang a knocker, and after a few long moments, a nun in full habit heaves the door open. She's holding a riding crop, and she's frowning.

Songs start running through my head and the Burning Days feel like yesterday, with the shrines of our name-kin all smashed and inquisitors forcing our ancestors to accept the Nameless God and speak the Wealdan tongue or face the pyre.

"Another straggler." The nun sighs and steps aside so the constables can carry-drag me in. "I'll take it from here, officers."

The constables let me loose, and one respectfully murmurs "Sister Gunnhild" as he tips his hat. My upper arms throb where the brutes gripped harder than they needed to, and my legs have gone watery after all those days on my rump. The massive door makes a deep, ominous thud as it closes, and the nun steps past to me to secure three complicated locks, one after the other after the other.

Locks that look hard to defeat. Locks that are likely on every door leading out of this place.

"Best get you accounted for," says Sister Gunnhild. "Follow me."

Five days in a prison wagon. Nothing to eat but bread and ale, like they don't know that Wealdan food will make me queasy. I just want a bed and a decent plate of broccoli.

But the nun demands an act of compliance too. They all do. Constables, landlords, inquisitors, tax collectors.

Graycoats.

I fold my arms and shake my head, even as my legs are seconds from dissolving and my belly churns like a boiling kettle.

Sister Gunnhild turns her eyes skyward like she's asking her Nameless God for patience. "I'll say this only once. All of this"—she gestures around the dim entryway—"the Crown is doing for your benefit. At a considerable cost to the taxpayers, too. Many of whom petitioned against the reforms allowing your lot this opportunity, as they think it's wasted on you. So behave yourself and things will go well for you. You won't like what happens if you can't manage that."

I hold my pose. Just a little longer. It's not compliance if it's exhaustion.

The nun sighs impatiently and whacks her riding crop against her palm, lip curled. I don't take my eyes off that razor-thin curve of leather. She'll aim for my haunch, too. Like I'm a horse. It will sting like blazes and draw blood and I will cry in front of a Wealdan like my parents said never to do.

"Ungovernable girls," Sister Gunnhild mutters. "Not worth the rope to hang 'em."

My heart flutters, because I'm not sure I heard her right. *Ungovernable* is an old word that I've heard no one but Master Grenallan say, and only when telling stories of Milea as it fell, stories about the men and women and girls like me who fought to keep it ours. Wealdans meant it to be shaming, but when Master Grenallan said it, there was a cheeky mocking that took out the sting, like the word belonged to him now and meant something new. Like all of us in hedge school should do small, mostly harmless, noncompliant things just so Wealdans would call us ungovernable.

At length Sister Gunnhild calls, "Bluebell! Lilac!"

Two novices appear. They're not much older than me, but training to be a nun must age you, because they stand without the slightest bit of curiosity or good cheer, like graycoats in a firing line.

"This girl requires our guidance," Sister Gunnhild says to them in a tight voice. "Escort her to intake."

Novice Lilac and Novice Bluebell hustle me down the hallway to a small wood-paneled room. There's a fat book on the lectern and a worn spot on the floor where the novices put me. Sister Gunnhild opens the book, flips a few pages, then takes up a pen and dips it in ink. "Where are you from? Do please answer. I would prefer not to give anyone demerits on her first day."

It's the *please* that gets me. It's one thing to be made to kneel and plead like my grands all had to. Another thing entirely to do what I'm asked.

I shake off the novices and say, "Trelawney Crossing. Lavender Province."

Sister Gunnhild looks up abruptly. "Your parents are

those terrorists! The ones who smashed the grain threshers and set all those horrible fires."

I nod once and swallow hard because even though I might cry for my ma and da, I won't do it in front of a nun. Instead I square up and reply, "After Lord and Lady Gaude evicted us."

"My brother and his two little children burned to death in the parlor of Highworthy Hall. Right in their own home." The nun grips her pen like a weapon. "All those lovely historic manor houses, gone forever. Along with good, decent people who gave your kind an honest day's work! Your rotten baby-killing parents ought to be hanging in chains right now. Dying slowly, day by desperate day."

Only the Crown doesn't martyr Mileans anymore. The Wealdans learned that lesson well enough—there's nothing to be gained from horror-show executions but more singers and more songs. They figured out there are worse punishments, especially for a people who hold their babies so close.

Their mas and das, too.

"And no one was *evicted*." Sister Gunnhild scowls. "Evictions have been illegal for years, and there won't be any slander in my school, especially not of the nobility."

"It's not slander if it's true," I mutter.

The nun's face goes pinchy-fierce. "You can still be sent to the workhouse. That most definitely can be arranged."

She's bluffing. She has to be. It was proven conclusively at trial that I had no hand in the machine breaking or the arson, that the worst thing I've ever done is fail to report my parents to the magistrates for keeping me out of national school. That's a fining offense, not a prison offense.

Not a death sentence.

"The judge said he'd be watching my case with interest," I reply, and it's a lot calmer than I feel. "The newspapers all reported where I got sent. Someone will notice if I'm disappeared."

"Perhaps." Sister Gunnhild stabs her pen at the book a few times, and I shiver because I get the sense she'd really rather be stabbing me. "Let's get on with it. Your name."

"Malliane Pirine Vinnio Aurelia Hesperus."

Sister Gunnhild scowls, then flips to the front of the book and runs a finger down the page. "Malliane is third on the list of prohibited names. Hmph. Be grateful unauthorized births no longer carry a sentence of correctional servitude. Your new name is Kem."

"No—it's Malley," I insist, because I can't have heard her right. A kem is a greasy Wealdan meat pie served to hired farm laborers.

But the nun merely scritches her pen across the page, blows on the ink, and lays the pen aside. "Now take down your hair."

I clap both hands over my topknot.

"You can take it down or we will cut it off."

Novice Bluebell pulls a huge pair of shears out of her pocket and shinks them open and closed. I'm panicking, but I force trembling fingers into my piled braids. One by one, I untie the ribbons and slip them into my pocket. There are a lot of things worth resisting, but without my braids I won't have any right to my name. I'll dishonor Malliane, the girl who made our name holy when she refused to empty a chamber pot for a Wealdan lady and died thirsty and raving, bound to a pole in her town's public square two generations before I was born. We are all named for someone on the Roll of Honor now, those fighters and rebels who met their end at Wealdan hands for some act of resistance. The Burning Days shattered families, and the workhouse did its best to finish them off. Sharing ungovernable names brings all Mileans into one big family, and even if you have no one else, you always have your name-kin.

I blink back tears. Everyone else's hair will be unbound. The grands went through much worse. I can replait my braids in the right pattern once I'm not here anymore, but with no hair at all, I'll have nothing to bind and Malliane won't recognize me as her own. She'll turn her back on me, and without name-kin I won't be Milean anymore.

All my pigtails tumble down. It feels like surrender. It feels like failure. Like the sidelong disgust of every Wealdan inquisitor who insists it's *idolatry* to revere men and women and girls like me who were done away with for resisting. Like Malliane is already wondering if I'm worthy of her name.

"Hurry," snaps Sister Gunnhild.

I unplait my pigtails one after another. Little pieces of binding twine litter the floor at my feet like dead worms. I can barely breathe. My hair is heavy, like a rippling sheaf of barley, and when I'm finished, it's floating everywhere like it hasn't since I was too small to remember.

The nun nods briskly. "If your hair is discovered bound in any way, it will be cut off. Shorn to the scalp. No warnings. No exceptions."

Novice Lilac holds out a handkerchief. This must be when a lot of girls start crying. Boys, too, maybe, at whatever schools they get sent to. I feel empty enough, but I cried myself out during the trial. That's probably what *really* kept me off the penal colony transport ship.

"Right, then, you're done." Sister Gunnhild turns to the novices. "She's number 1076. Get her a uniform and take her to holding."

"A *uniform*?" My mouth falls open and I forget to look her in the feet. "But this is school! Not the workhouse! I thought . . ." But I can't say what I thought, because my throat has closed all the way up, and it doesn't matter anyway. No one here is going to care what I think.

Novice Bluebell holds out her hand. I'm about to collapse and a hand is almost like a *please*, so I go where she points, through a long, dark hallway that slopes down and down and doesn't seem to end.

• • •

My uniform is a gown. A gown! With my unbound hair, it's a wonder a diaper isn't part of this silly costume. In a little room lined with shelves of white clothing, Novice Bluebell explains how to put on the gown and tie a length of cord around my waist. When I ask why, she says it makes a girl look like a girl.

A Wealdan girl, they mean. Sweet and prim and tidy, perfect for looking at. Not strong from cranking the cider press or clever enough to fix both kinds of plow.

Novice Lilac gives me other clothes to wear with the gown. There's an undershift, a set of stockings, and a pair of drawers, and everything is made of coarse, undyed wool straight off a sheep's back. My hands start to itch just holding them. All of the clothing—even the underpants—has the empire's ridiculous overwrought crest stamped on it. Both novices give me a *hurry up* look, so I sigh, strip down to my nothing, and pull the shift over my head. Right away I can feel a rash in the shape of the Embattled Crown digging into my skin. As I finish dressing, Novice Lilac uses a fireplace poker to pick up my comfortable old shirt and trousers and shove them into a rucksack.

"My ribbons!" I grab for my trousers, where I shoved the strips of silk from my topknot, but Novice Lilac cinches the rucksack closed and pulls it out of reach.

"Since you haven't been told the rules yet, I'm going to pretend I didn't hear that," Novice Bluebell says. "Tie your belt, all right?"

"Please." I'm begging and it turns my stomach, but I can't lose one more thing today. "I won't wear them. I just want to have them."

Novice Lilac smiles big and false. "We'll make sure you get everything you need to be successful here. All you have to do is follow the rules."

"Your new clothes are in this trunk—uniforms, stockings, underwear, nightgowns—so keep them neatly folded in here." Novice Bluebell nudges a wooden box with leather handles toward me. "There's a complete outfit for each day of the week, so you'll put on a clean uniform every morning. Everything's numbered, see? 1076. That's you."

First my plaits. Now my ribbons. My ancestors went through worse, so I have enough songs to know what to do. Chin up. Stand square. Blank your gaze. Whatever else, do not cry. This is how you resist. This is how you stay Milean.

Novice Lilac steps into the corridor. "Now pick up your trunk and come along."

Bad enough I'll have to wear this stuff. Now I have to haul it too. I heave the trunk up by the straps and lurch behind the novices out of the uniform alcove, down more stairs and ramps, till Novice Bluebell pulls a chunky iron key from her pocket and grates it into the biggest lock I've ever seen.

"Holding," she says. "In you go."

The holding area is a chilly, echoing chamber with a

handful of narrow iron beds lined up like graycoats in formation, all empty but made up and waiting. Besides a balcony and a closed wooden door that must open to it, there's nothing else in the room but sturdy, plain sconces on the walls, glowing with what must be gaslight, although I only know about gaslight from hedge school.

"Am I the last one?" I don't bother to hide a proud smirk. "The last Milean kid in the province to end up here?"

"One of the last." Novice Lilac says it accusingly, like I should feel ashamed that my parents sent me to hide in the greenwood when the Crown's school wagons neared Trelawney Crossing.

A Milean girl steps onto the balcony. She has a shining curtain of brown hair and she's wearing a gown like mine, only with a red scarf around her neck that dangles almost to her waist. I'm so happy to see another Milean that I shout "Kyora!" before I remember not to.

"Outlawed tongue." Novice Lilac digs a pad of paper out of her pocket. "That's a demerit. Better watch yourself. We count even while you're in holding."

The girl on the balcony doesn't look down, either at my greeting or my outburst. She stares straight ahead, even though there's nothing but wall for her to talk to, and says in Wealdan, "I am Loe, appointed cantor of this session by Sister Gunnhild. It is springtide in the seventh year of the reign of our illustrious sovereign. Long and glorious may he rule."

She doesn't trip over the words or mangle them. She sounds like she actually wishes him well. This is what they make of us here. This is what they want to make of *me*.

Novice Bluebell glances up at the Milean girl, then nods to Novice Lilac and they head toward the big door.

"What's going on?" I put the trunk down. "Why am I here? When is *supper*, at least?"

"These are the behavioral expectations while a girl takes part in a course of study at the Forswelt National School," says the Milean girl, still talking to the wall.

"There are no open fourth-rank beds right now," Novice Lilac tells me. "You'll stay in holding till that changes. Meals will be brought three times a day. While you're here, you're expected to listen to the cantor and learn what's required."

"But—"

The door slams behind the novices, and outside there's the scrape of a key in a lock.

"Forswelt's operation is based on the chamber," the Milean girl says. "There are four girls to a chamber, one of each rank. Girls of the fourth rank have no privileges and must earn them with compliance. Privileges escalate until a girl reaches the first rank, when she has the most prestige and freedom the school has to offer."

I swivel and peer up at the cantor, then move to the middle of the holding area to get a better view. She's not squirming in her uniform like I am. Just wearing this dress stamped with the Embattled Crown makes it seem like I belong to the empire somehow. I want to hide under a bed already, even though there's no one here to see me but this girl.

"Hey!" I shout. "Down here!"

"Students spend even days in the classroom," the girl goes on, "and on odd days, they engage in the vocational training that will prepare them for a successful future."

"Will you please just listen for a minute?"

But Cantor Loe just keeps reciting garbage about uniforms—*girls will wear a complete set of Crown-issued clothing at all times, and any altering or defacing of these garments will result in disciplinary action*—and peer monitoring—*girls will receive rewards in various forms every time they report another student for behavior that violates our community standards or any school rule.* When she gets to the part about decorum—*students will refer to nuns with the title of honora and novices as honorata,* like they're inquisitors or factory bosses or collectors of the monthly tithes—I turn away and flop on the bed nearest the door.

It's like lying on fence rails. Nothing at all like the gentle sway of a hammock. My throat starts to close and I bite my lip hard, but it's too late. Treacherous, unsongworthy things appear in my head one by one. *I should have just turned myself in. Then I'd have been sent to the same school as my friends instead of this far-distant one. At least I wouldn't be alone right now. It's not compliance if it's plain good sense.*

This is why the likes of Everard and Jasperine have songs about them and I never will. This is why my ma and da never once woke me on the cold mornings they'd disappear into the mist with their crowbars and cudgels and jugs of kerosene, even though I kept making them promise they would. This is why Milea fell in the first place and now we live somewhere called New Weald. In the old days, flying columns of rebels made guerrilla raids on Wealdan landlords and inquisitors. They fought back to back, outnumbered, surrounded, scythes against rifles. This is why I can't fall apart at national school. I have to survive it as Malley and not end up this Kem person the Wealdans decided I should be.

Magistrates were always telling mas and das in Trelawney Crossing how national school was a victory, how they should be grateful that the new sovereign was modern and progressive and chose to implement reforms that would improve the lives of New Wealdan children across the provinces. Only it didn't sound like victory when the school wagons rolled up. Even deep in the greenwood where I was hiding, I could hear kids bawling. Grown-ups, too. Sharp and shrieking, like waterbirds when hunters come upon them, or deep and grinding like a dying bear. This would be the last time they'd see one another for a whole year, and only if kids behaved well enough to earn a visit. If parents came on school grounds for any reason, the whole family would be sent to the workhouse. The kids crying was bad enough, but that was nothing compared with how the grown-ups wept once the wagon creaking faded. It was days and days before the village was calm enough for me to risk coming back.

Master Grenallan did what he could to prepare us. I knew to expect filling, regular meals and the company of only girls and women. I knew there'd be warm beds and medical treatment if I got sick and some kind of formal instruction. But I also knew about the locks and walls. I knew I'd be spending more hours inside than out, and the only sunlight I'd see would be whatever managed to trickle through window glass.

"You won't be there alone," he'd say. "You'll have one another." Which would have been true if I'd let the Wealdans send me to the school nearest my village. Instead I have these girls who might not have had a schoolmaster like mine or a ma and da who were pushed into resisting. But chances are good these girls heard the same speeches from their magistrates. Sobbed as they climbed into school wagons. Felt only a handsbreadth tall when assigned a uniform like some sort of criminal and made to listen to rule after rule after rule, when at home they likely had the same three I did: have a decent attitude, don't get in trouble with the law, and do chores to keep the homestead running.

Above me, the cantor goes on about structure and order. Sister Gunnhild wouldn't have complained about ungovernable girls if I was the only one. Maybe Master

Grenallan was right and I'm not alone here after all. Maybe some of these girls feel their ancestors' blessings on their heads too. Staying Milean in this place will be so much easier if I'm not the only one trying to hold on to everything that makes me who I am.

INSTEAD OF BRINGING BREAKFAST AS USUAL,
Novice Bluebell turns up with a long scarf knitted from
coarse orange yarn. "A fourth-rank bed opened up. Here,
put this on and come with me."

Cantor Loe is still speaking up in her balcony. By now,
I can recite the rules along with her. That's probably the
point. I wave, since it seems polite after all this time, but
Novice Bluebell stands to like a graycoat.

"The cantor is not here to be engaged," she snaps. "278
didn't interact with you, did she?"

I shake my head.

"You managed to get several demerits here in holding,"
Novice Bluebell says. "If the cantor did try to speak with

you directly and you were to tell me, some of those demerits would go away."

Girls advance through the four ranks by means of a merit system. Each day that a girl participates in class and vocational training incident free moves her closer to achieving a better rank. Demerits may be assigned for any infraction a girl commits, minor or serious, and they will slow her progression through the ranks. In some cases, amassing enough demerits may make her lose a rank, and it will have to be earned back.

If a girl receives a total of thirty or more demerits, she will be assigned a correctional vocational opportunity to provide intensive instruction on the virtue of compliance. If she earns a second such opportunity, she will be sent to the workhouse, as it will be clear that the first one taught her nothing.

I shake my head again. The inquisitors did this too. There were rewards aplenty for anyone who reported a neighbor with a shrine to her name-kin or gave evidence at morality court.

Novice Bluebell hands me the scarf, and I loop it around my neck. It's softer than it looks and an actual color, which cheers me up considerably. Then I pick up my trunk, and she leads me out of the holding area and down a hallway past a line of girls scrubbing a series of wooden doors with something that smells sharp and bleachy. Not one glances up from her work as we pass, and their flurries and curtains and frizzes of unbound hair hide their faces. They're not wearing scarves, either, which is against the rules—*girls must wear scarves in the color corresponding with their rank at all times during waking hours*—which makes me grin outright. Maybe these girls are resisting. Maybe school won't be as bad as I thought.

"Good idea," I murmur to the girl nearest to me as I reach for my scarf. "I'm going to ditch mine, too." I try to catch her eye as I do it, but she just stoops to dunk her scrub brush in a bucket of murky water.

"That's a demerit," Novice Bluebell says to me sternly. "Take off your scarf and you'll find yourself with *five*."

The girl doesn't have gloves. None of them do. Their hands are scabby and peeling from the cleaner.

Something cold turns over in my belly.

I leave my scarf alone and move away from the girls, falling into step behind Novice Bluebell. Before long, we get to the residence wing and the novice winds down corridors until we stand in front of a door labeled with a squiggle of Wealdan numerals. She pushes it open. The door's not locked or even latched. The walls are whitewashed, and there's a cat-size window near the ceiling, covered with a sturdy grate. There are four beds in a line, trunks at the foot of all but one, and enough room between everything for someone to walk. Three girls in uniforms like mine are tugging sheets and pulling up blankets, leaning across the narrow frames to make everything precise and even. Each wears a different scarf—red, green, and blue. The green-scarf girl looks to be the oldest, and her straw-straight black hair swishes in a sheet past her waist. The blue-scarf girl is strong and solid, like a dairymaid, and has hair the color of old honey. The red-scarf girl looks like my ma must have when she was young, round and curvy and chin-up fearless. When we walk in, they all stop making their beds and stand at attention in front of their trunks.

"1076 is your new fourth," Novice Bluebell tells them. "Three demerits."

The blue-scarf girl muffles a groan, but the red-scarf girl says, "Yes, honorata. Understood."

Once the novice leaves, the girls relax visibly and break from their poses, and so do I. When they're not standing to like a row of foreign dolls, it's easier to imagine them as girls from my village who I might have been friends with once upon a time.

"Put away your things." The green-scarf girl points to where my trunk should go, at the bottom of the bare pallet bed where there's a neatly folded parcel that looks to be linens. "We'll help you with the covers."

"It can't matter that much, can it?" I drop my trunk where I'm standing. "I won't even be sleeping in it till tonight."

The blue-scarf girl sighs long and loud. "Why do I always get stuck with the malcontents?"

"Tal. No one wants to fail room inspection, right?" The green-scarf girl pulls apart the bed-linen parcel and flings the bottom sheet over the thin pallet while the red-scarf girl tucks it under. "I'm Sab. That's Fee."

The red-scarf girl, Fee, nods at me as she and Sab whip the woolen blankets tight and plop down a pillow.

"Do we really have to use these imperial names?" I roll my eyes. "Even when it's just us?"

Sab nods firmly. "Someone's always listening. I can't get any more demerits, especially for something stupid like a language violation."

My mouth falls open to list the martyrs who slid their heads through links of massive white-hot chains rather than utter so much as a syllable in the Wealdan tongue.

Fee smiles wryly and gestures to the front of my gown. "Numbers are worse. Just tell us what we can call you."

She's right. Wealdans think in numbers and maps and paper documents, posting them on chapel doors and pointing to them in land grabs and presenting them at morality court like their simple existence makes them binding and valid. I choke on the word Sister Gunnhild chose for me, though. It's not a name. It's not *me*.

They wait, but when I stare hard at the ground, Sab and Fee and Tal herd me out of the room and down the corridor, talking about breakfast. I let myself be herded. All the novices brought me to eat in the holding area were sandwiches made with heavy Wealdan bread, and I'm desperate for a salad.

The dining hall is full of square tables, each with four wooden chairs, and when my chambermates sit together at one, I follow their lead. A dozen novices patrol the room, and this lot looks far more sullen than Bluebell or Lilac. There's food somewhere nearby, lots of it, fried okra and sizzling asparagus and tofu and fresh rain-dappled lettuce tossed into a big colorful salad. Actual decent-smelling food that might almost be mistaken for something my da would make.

Tal and Fee and Sab shift in their chairs. Already I wish I could take back how I acted in the chamber, how rude I was and how I didn't even help make my own bed. They must think I'm some sort of prance-around ninny. I'm going to be stuck here for years. I'm not going to spend that time knuckling under, and I want these girls on my side.

"Kem," I tell them in a low voice. "You can call me Kem."

A woman in a gray gown taps a bell and calls, "First rank!"

The only sound in the room is chairs scraping the floor as girls in red scarves rise and line up at a series of trestles at one end of the dining hall. Cantor Loe must have repeated fifty times how girls in the first rank have the most privileges, but it took me three repetitions to figure out what a *privilege* is—there's no word like it in Milean—and another few to understand that I'm supposed to believe something earned with compliance is a good thing.

Fee returns with a heaping pile of roasted cauliflower, a huge baked potato, a slab of vegetable scramble, and a bowl of sprouts and greens dappled with spices. I can't take my eyes off that spread. So they *do* know what vegetables are at Forswelt. They know exactly what Milean food ought to look like. The second rank is called next, and Tal brings back a plate heaped with the dregs of the vegetable scramble, a wedge of cheese, and a bowl of meat broth with soggy-looking onion and carrot shreds. I'm more than a little worried when Sab returns with a plate of noodles in parsnip sauce, and by the time the fourth rank is called and I get to the head of the line, there's nothing left but sandwiches.

Bread and meat. *Again.*

I take a single sandwich with two pinchy fingers, like it's dirty. It looks small on my tray. I've got to eat something, but too much bread and I'll get grainsick, and I don't think I can be any kind of sick without my ma to make me ginger tea and warm my blankets by the fire and nudge my hammock with her foot so it sways just the smallest, calming, comforting bit.

Back at the table, I station my breakfast in front of me and take a deep breath. The sandwich bread is damp. It smells a bit like shoes, which makes me suspicious of the meat inside. There's a smushy yellow goo as well. I peel the bread apart and touch the inside to my tongue. The yellow stuff doesn't taste too bad. It's not vegetables, but—

"Kem!" Sab whispers sharply. "Knock it off and eat before the novices see!"

"Whuh?" My tongue is still on the bread. "There's rules for how I have to *eat* as well?"

"You can't waste food," Tal says. "You have to finish everything you take."

"Best reason to make third rank." Fee smiles sympathetically and nods at my plate, then casually forks a bite of spicy greens into her mouth. I know they're spicy because I can smell them from here, even over the leathery whiff of the bread. Apparently, eating actual food is a privilege that has to be earned with compliance, which means each of my chambermates is doing as she's told without fuss or protest—Fee most of all, if she's first rank.

"No," I whisper, because maybe I *am* alone here. Maybe there's nothing to do but wear a babyish gown with the empire's stupid crest and behave myself so things go well for me and only cry for my ma and da under my covers long after the lights go out.

"Kem, what are you *doing*?"

I look down. I've squished the sandwich in my fist. Worms of soggy bread and meat and yellow spread curl between my fingers. I open my hand and flick the mess onto my plate. "How can you all go along with this? Someone's going to get grainsick! Haven't you ever been freaking grainsick before? Haven't you seen someone *die* from it?"

A nudge to my ribs. It's Sab, and she's panicking. "Just eat, Kem! Please! We're in enough trouble. You're only making it worse."

Two novices are threading through the dining hall, demerit pads already in hand. Fee and Tal look like they're chewing live bees. I wipe my hands on a napkin and pick up one of the less nasty pieces of sandwich so it at least looks like I'm eating, even though I can't imagine why my chambermates would care if I got in trouble.

"One demerit for bad language," the taller novice says. "Two for slander, and another four for conspiracy."

I lift my chin. This is when someone else will speak up. Someone else could well become everyone else. We've all seen what happens to Mileans who can't afford the garden tax and have to survive on Wealdan bread from the markets.

"*Conspiracy?*" Sab wails. "I don't want that on my record!"

"Seven demerits," Tal mutters. "On top of the three you brought us. Unbelievable."

I turn to face her. "Wait. What do you mean, *the three I brought you?*"

"She's going to eat it," Fee says to the red-cheeked novice writing primly on her pad.

The novice ignores Fee and frowns at Sab. "You're perilously close to losing a rank, 145."

Sab's eyes fill with angry tears.

"But they didn't do anything!" I feel bellysick and I haven't eaten a bite. "I'm the one who—"

"Shut *up*," Tal hisses. "You've done enough."

"As for the rest of you," the taller novice says, gesturing with her scribbled-on pad, "if you don't like 1076 racking up demerits for you, you'd best make sure she learns the rules. Quickly."

Fee, Sab, and Tal mutter, "Yes, honorata," while I glare at my ruined sandwich and try to keep from crying. It's not like I expected my chambermates to tell off the novices—even if the Relief Act took some of the worst abuses off the books, challenging a Wealdan never comes consequence free—but they could have stood up for me, at least a little. They could have stood up for themselves, and for every girl in this room who has to risk getting grainsick when there are clearly enough vegetables to go around.

"Do you get it now?" Tal asks bitterly.

I nod. I'm trembling. Anytime I step out of line and get demerits, my entire chamber will end up with them too.

The gray-gown lady rings the bell and girls throughout the room push back their chairs and leave the dining hall in a stream of white dresses and unbound hair. They leave their dishes, too, like none of their mas or das ever made them come in from playing to clear a forgotten plate or mug. I follow my chambermates down a gaslit corridor. My stomach's so twisty-sloshy it's hard to do anything more complicated. I can't look at these girls. Any of them. Not a one has said a cross word to me, but they're doing what the nuns want without even a whisper of resistance.

Maybe I'm alone here now, but there's no reason I have to stay that way. These girls have been stuck at school longer. They've forgotten what it is to wear trousers and sleep

in hammocks and look people in the eye. They've forgotten
what a songworthy act even is. Maybe they didn't have as
much hedge school as I did. Maybe none at all, if their
parents couldn't bear the risk. Chances are good they never
had Master Grenallan to wink and smirk and remind them
to be ungovernable. They likely don't even know *how* to
resist. If not for my ma and da, I'd be just like them. These
girls are asleep, and I won't be worthy of my name if I let
them stay that way.

We end up in a long hallway lined with doors, and I follow Fee and Sab and Tal into a room that's bare and whitewashed like everything else in this place. There are perhaps
thirty girls clustered four to a table. Chambermates, probably, like we are. This must be a classroom, and I can't help
but look toward the window, though all I can see is a muddy
yard with a pump and not a fragrant, prickly hedge.

Maybe the window opens. Maybe just a breeze would
be enough.

The nun at the front of the room is young and rosy-
cheeked, but her expression as she looks us over is absolutely venomous. When we're all seated, she snaps, "First
rank."

Fee and the other red-scarf girls go to a shelf at the back,
where they each retrieve a book covered in brown paper.
When the fourth rank is finally called, the only remaining books are tattered, and they're all different sizes, so
I have no idea which one I'm supposed to choose. I only

know what books are because Master Grenallan told us the Wealdans write everything down and don't bother to memorize anything.

Books look flimsy. They look fragile and flammable.

We may have lost the ancestors to the pyre and the grands to the workhouses, but the songs are all in my head because memory is the only place where something so precious can truly be safe.

"Crogen!"

I flinch. I can't help it. I flinch and then fist up both hands because I should be used to that slur and I'm not, and I have to let out a long steady breath like my da taught me instead of pouring out the rude retort that would open my back under a whip.

The nun prods my haunch impatiently with a riding crop. When I turn, she sighs. "Oh. The new girl. I clearly don't have enough to do without you being dumped in my lap. Well, get a primer and get to work."

"What's a primer?" I gesture at the shelf.

She brings the crop down hard across my fingers. I suck in a breath and clutch my stinging hand to my chest.

"Try. *Again.*" Her eyes are narrow, her scowl vicious.

I grit back tears. The other girls are bent over their books, even my chambermates. A few sneak glances at me sidelong, but none of them is helpful.

"I don't—ow!"

The nun smacks my thighs—twice—fast—and I stumble

backward, out of reach. She aims the crop at me and growls, "If no one's taught you manners, I will. You want to speak to me? Don't. If you have to speak *of* me, it's Sister Chlotilde. Also? Don't you *ever* look me in the eye again." Then she grabs a book off the shelf and slams it into my belly, sending me staggering. "This is a primer. A *pri-mer*. Now go sit with those other dimwits and don't make another sound till I say you can."

I clutch the book with aching hands and stumble back to my seat beside Tal. Sister Chlotilde watches me go like I just peed on her shoes, then clumps back to her desk and sits down with a newspaper.

She's like the inquisitors, then. At least now I know where I stand. You resist inquisitors at your peril.

Books are a mystery to me, but this one has clearly seen better days. The pages are dirty and smudged, and they dangle from the center where they're stitched together. Sab has her book open to the middle. I do likewise, but Fee discreetly reaches across the table and flips the pages back to the beginning. The first one has a series of symbols in three neat rows. On each of the pages that follow, there's a single symbol and a picture.

I have no idea what to make of it. Little kids must learn this stuff in lower school now, but Master Grenallan never mentioned it. Chances are good I'll get whacked again if I don't at least pretend, so I turn pages. The pictures are interesting. I like them. The first one is an animal of some kind with orange fur and a long, slinky tail. Then a smiling Wealdan baby sitting in an oval pen dressed in a ruffly gown and surrounded by factory-made toys and frilly blankets.

The next one is a graycoat standing at attention with his rifle at his shoulder, bayonet sharp and ready, and the classroom falls away and it's the Sutherland Fair and the music and chatter stop abruptly as a magistrate barks out the Assembly Restriction Act, but the graycoats don't wait for the fairgoers to comply and bayonets catch sunlight as they slash and stab till they're too gummed with blood and my small sticky hand gets wrenched out of Da's and the screaming—

Fee reaches over and turns the page so fast it's a blur.

The next picture is a flowery meadow, and I pull in breath after breath while the classroom grows back around me, brick by whitewashed brick.

It's just a picture.

My da found me eventually. I have no memory of being shut in a kennel *for my own safety*. He wasn't even mad about having to pay that sly-handed Wealdan merchant to let me out.

It's just a picture.

Most of the blood wasn't mine. The bruises all faded. The nightmares mostly went away.

I swallow hard and close my eyes and sing outlawed songs in my head till I can be here again in this room with these girls.

Time crawls by. The room is perfectly silent but for the soft rustling of pages being turned. The gaslight whooshes and crackles. My legs ache from the sitting, from being crimped in a wooden chair, and my thighs still throb from the crop. A leaf blows across the mud in the yard and sticks to the pump.

This is nothing like hedge school, where Master Grenallan would ask us questions about edible plants or how to spot a flaw in someone's reasoning and we'd all fling our hands in the air with the hope he'd call on us. He'd have each of us rise and share the story of our name-kin, who we could no longer honor openly. We'd sing the old songs and the new songs and recite the Roll of Honor so every last one of us, down to the tiniest kid who toddled up holding a bigger kid's hand, would remember who had tried to keep our homeland and what had befallen them for it.

"Intermediate readers." Sister Chlotilde's voice is bored. "Rise and read from *Willa the Happy Factory Girl*. Don't make me use the crop."

Girls with all different colored scarves form a line along one side of the classroom. I sit up straighter. This is more like it. No ranks. No privileges to set us against one another.

The first girl opens her book and clears her throat. "Willa works at the porcelain factory. She paints flowers on the teacups with a cute, tiny brush. When—"

"Shut up, you're done," Sister Chlotilde cuts in. "Next. Hurry this up."

"When the foreman says the girls must work overtime," the second girl reads, "Willa is happy because she knows the glory of the em . . . empee—"

"*Empire.*" Sister Chlotilde sighs hard enough to scatter her bangs. "Any fool knows that! Sit down and stop wasting my time."

The intermediate readers keep going one after another. I hate Willa the brain-dead factory girl before they're even halfway done with the story. Willa is grateful to the Crown for her job, and she would never risk losing it by complaining or doing poor work. Twelve-hour shifts are no problem for a sturdy New Wealdan girl like her! When her painting hand starts to hurt or she gets dizzy from the fumes, she thinks how her work appears on tables across the empire, and that makes it all worthwhile. She knows boys are trouble and plans never to marry or have children—the empire needs her at work, and she will devote her life to it. She chooses not to associate with bad influences that might lead her off the path of right living that she learned from the nuns at her beloved national school. If all books are this full of rubbish, they can stay a mystery.

A bell rings somewhere outside, like a clock tower, and Sister Chlotilde slams both palms on her desk and groans, "Finally! Now get out, all of you, and leave me in peace."

The girls put their books back on the shelf and file out of the classroom. No sidelong sneers in her direction. No rolling their eyes. Sister Chlotilde rattles her newspaper open and deliberately blocks us out with it, so I make a rude face at her as I pass her desk. Sab and Tal are already gone. I put my primer away and wait for Fee, but she doesn't exactly look happy to see me.

"Lunch," she says briskly, nodding me down the corridor.

I trot at her elbow. I have so many questions. "This is what we'll be stuck doing here? Reading? From *books*?"

Fee plows down the hall, not looking at me. "There's no reading group beyond advanced. After that, you start learning deportment and something they call civics. Basically, why the empire is so great and why you should love it."

"I suppose we'll be made to learn to write, too," I mutter.

"Nah. The nuns are pretty sure we can barely manage reading. They don't want to make us do things that are too hard for us. They say its bad for our adjustment."

"But what—"

"We'll get demerits if we discuss our studies," Fee cuts in. "No offense, but I don't want any."

I almost ask how the nuns would even know, but it doesn't matter. What matters is that Fee believes it. Everyone seems to. *Someone's always listening.* Instead I say, "You have to help me do something about this place."

Fee smiles, strained and polite. "Kem . . . look, you just got here. It's hard. The rules. The scarves. The ranks. I won't inform on you, but you can't talk like that. It's better to do what they say. Not because you buy into it. Because it's easier."

"No. That can't be right. We're Milean. That's not what we do. That's not what *I'm* going to do."

"Really?" There's an edge to Fee's voice. "You're going to take us down with you, then. Three girls who never did anything to you. You'll drag us all below or land us in the workhouse."

The workhouse. Where we'll be stripped and shorn and herded into a big walled yard with desperate men and women, and every night we survive, we'll be rewarded the next morning with a pickax or a boning knife and eighteen hours' hard labor down a mine or in a slaughterhouse or on a road crew. The longest anyone's ever lasted is five months, and he only lived that long by turning cannibal and burying the gnawed-clean bones of other inmates in the privy trough until parasites finished him off. The woodcuts of the scene from the newspapers the inquisitors posted on the chapel doors gave me nightmares for weeks.

Fee could be exaggerating, or wrong, or simply a knuckle-under, but I can't help asking, "Below?"

"How many demerits do you have now?" she asks. "Ten at least, and they should have told you what happens when you get to thirty."

"Some vocational thing, right?" I shrug, but I'm starting to feel bellysick. "Everyone has to do vocational training."

"This isn't training. This is basically the workhouse in the basement of our school."

I fold my arms and try to look unimpressed, but that word gives me shudders and songs start going through my head and Fee has to be wrong because the Education Act states exactly how Milean children spend their time while in the Crown's care.

"Who do you think is behind all the food that appears in the dining hall three times a day and the clean dishes we eat off?" Fee asks. "Those tidy parcels of bed linens? Shiny-scrubbed floors and wash stations that aren't all moldy and foul? The tables cleared after we eat? Girls who've been sent below who you never see. Girls you never *will* see."

The inquisitors did this too. Tried to convince us how a terrible fate awaited nonbelievers, how our survival in this world and the next depended on complete obedience both to the Nameless God's teachings and the leadership of his chosen representatives, all of whom happened to be Wealdans who profited from our land and labor.

Yet that first day I was hustled past girls with no scarves scrubbing doors—the only girls with no scarves I've seen since I left holding.

"Also?" Fee gets right in my face. "Your demerits go away at a quarter of the regular time when you're below, so it takes four times as long to work them off. That's the official line, anyway. No one knows, because girls never seem to work off those correctional sentences."

"All the more reason for us to resist!" I snap. "The nuns are breaking the rules—rules they made themselves!"

"All the more reason for you to stop getting so many demerits," Fee says, "because it's not against the Education Act for them to give us consequences when we mess up, and a *correctional vocational opportunity* is totally legal."

I press my hands against my eyes. I can't exactly tell Fee she's wrong for not wanting to go somewhere worse than school. "I'll try. I'm sorry. No one's told me what will get me demerits. I didn't even know all of you would get stuck with the demerits I earned. The cantor didn't say a word about it."

Fee grimaces. "She *couldn't*. The rules she's allowed to recite are just the ones they have to make public by statute. And don't spend too much time trying to figure out demerits. The nuns give them randomly on purpose."

Of course they do. The better to keep us compliant. If we never know what will happen if we step out of line, we're less likely to risk doing anything but what we're told.

"So there's nothing to be done, then," I mutter in disgust. "No wrecking Sister Chlotilde's precious newspaper. No tripping her in the hallway."

"You'd better be kidding about that," Fee replies through her teeth. "I do *not* want to end up in the workhouse because of you."

"They can't send someone there just because. It's against the law. The Education Act—"

"—says there are only three reasons a Milean child can be excluded from school and sent to the workhouse." Fee rubs her forehead like she's got a headache. "If you physically attack a nun or a novice. Tripping her in the hall, for instance. If you try to run away. Really, if you're outside school grounds and you're not with a nun or a novice. Or if you're caught singing a song."

My mouth falls open.

"Any song," Fee goes on, "in any language."

I must know a thousand-thousand songs about what happened as Milea was broken and ground down and spat out as New Weald—the ancestors bound on the pyre, the grands dragged to the workhouses, and anyone still standing made to work for starvation wages as tenants of new-made Wealdan landlords. There will be no songs here, though. No "Lament for Jasperine Vesley." No "Inquisitor Meets the Harrow." No "Everard's Flying Column." Songs are what make us Milean. Songs give us a place to celebrate survival and turn it into victory. They give us a place to resist. The schoolmasters knew this. That's why they made songs in the first place.

That's why the Wealdans went after schoolmasters first.

After the guilty verdict was handed down and the sentence passed, the judge allowed me to spend a day and a night with my parents in the guardhouse before they were put on the transport ship. A constable brought me from the detention center just hours after my ma and da had been branded with the Embattled Crown. Their scalps were more reddened bandages than skin and only random tufts of hair remained, and they slumped against each other like worn-out dolls. If this was a song, they'd have been standing defiant and taunting the constables—*Shaving our heads and branding us shoulder and haunch, is that the best you've got?*—and then I'd have known what to do. I'd have lifted my chin and my eyes would have glittered and I'd have promised to travel throughout the land, singing of their deeds so they would never be forgotten.

It wasn't a song, though. It was a dim earthwork guardhouse that smelled like cooked flesh and sweat. So I didn't know what to do. If I didn't look at my parents, I could remember them healthy and sun-browned and laughing. My da in his herb garden, carefully putting his big feet between the narrow, delicate rows. My ma with her weaving or carving, always busy, always making something. Those months on trial had withered my parents stringy and gray, even before they'd been marked as criminals. I clung to the doorframe, staring hard at my feet.

Then my ma edged a hand into her pocket, tugged loose a thick purple ribbon that used to be in her topknot, and held it out to me. In just over a day's time I'd never see my parents again. All we could do now was be together. I flew across the room and fell against my ma, and she pulled me close in slow, painful jerks. Her hug was still warm and powerful, though, and these last few embraces would have to keep me my whole life. My da shifted enough to put his arms around us both, and we stayed like that for ages. It must have been agony for them to hold me so long, given how their backs and backsides were still raw from the hot irons.

One of us eventually let go, and we broke apart to sit on the benches. It was early evening, and the night ahead began to feel like a torment instead of a blessing. Every moment that went by was one less we had together. I wove my ma's ribbon through my piled pigtails and she admired it and we pretended not to know why she didn't need it anymore. When my da asked if I was eating well, I made up elaborate lies about the food in the detention center.

Then it got quiet. We were trying for normal when nothing would ever be normal again.

So I started singing "Everard's Flying Column." If I didn't sing I'd cry, and that would have broken them for sure. After two verses I choked on a sob, but my da picked up the refrain and my ma joined the next verse and I found a way to keep singing. One by one, we sang the songs they remembered growing up and the songs I learned in hedge school. Songs they learned from the grands as the Burning Days ramped up, which the grands got from the ancestors as it became increasingly clear what Milea's fate was soon to be.

Jasperine with her rifle like a ghost in the greenwood, taking down graycoats one by one during the first evictions and bringing food to starving tenants in those miserable high-rent crofts. Everard at that snow-blistered pass, turning back a whole column of Wealdan cavalry with his band of thirty. Every great Milean has a song, and I know them all by heart. So many of the ancestors died believing their last acts of resistance were futile and forgettable. These songs prove them wrong. These songs mean men and women and girls like me can live forever.

At dawn my parents roused themselves from their bench. My ma wrapped her fist in the rest of the ribbons from her topknot and bashed the shutter out of the narrow airway at the top of the cell. My da made a step of his hands pressed together, and shoulder to branded shoulder they boosted me up and out and told me to stay free as long as I could.

Which turned out to be not very long, mostly because I couldn't help myself and went back to our old homestead, only it was being used as a stable and stupid fat show ponies were making a wreck of my ma's handmade rugs and maybe I got even by spooking them and scattering them to the four winds, which might have tipped off the constabulary.

I might know a thousand-thousand songs, but none of them are about girls who can't even keep themselves out of Wealdan prison school. None of them are about girls who comply a little more each day till they forget they've ever been anything but what the Wealdans would have them be.

• • •

After lunch, we trudge back to class. I catch up to Sab as we're pulling out our chairs. I've got a long way to go if I want my chambermates to tolerate me. Longer still if we're to be friends, and even longer before they'll wake up and resist alongside me.

"Hey, I'm sorry about what happened at breakfast," I tell Sab. "I was so hungry, and sandwiches are vile. I honestly didn't know all of you would get in trouble too."

Sab sighs. "Ten demerits, Kem. Who gets *ten demerits* on her first day?"

"To be fair, I only got seven today," I reply. "I barely remember where the others came from. Breathing wrong, probably. One was definitely for throwing a sandwich at the door of holding as one of the flower twins closed it."

Sab cracks a reluctant smile. "Sandwiches *are* vile. Only . . . go along with it, all right? There's no shame in surviving. Not all of us were given that chance."

She says it like she's still mourning someone who wasn't, so I study my felt shoes and keep my mouth shut. All these girls are doing just that—taking the chance they've been given. It's not their fault. It's what's meant to happen here. The Crown doesn't even pretend that's not the goal. It's the very first line in the Education Act.

"You are being *given* nothing," Master Grenallan would say. "You are being made to take something. It's not a choice if there's only one real option open to you."

I know to resist because Master Grenallan said I could. I loved him like an uncle and I cried for days when the graycoats disappeared him. The longer I'm at national school, the harder it will be to remember him. The harder it will be to stay Milean, especially if I'm the only one trying.

Sister Chlotilde calls us by ranks to get books. I know what to do this time so I don't get whacked on the knuckles, but somehow I'm going to have to get through a whole afternoon in this dead-still, airless room. It's not going to be easy.

I open the primer to the picture of the orange animal. Someone has drawn two halves of a nun hanging from its jaws. The nun's eyes are x-ed out and her guts are dribbling into a pool at the animal's feet, where the corpses of other nuns lie scattered.

I bite back a giggle.

The baby in its oval pen is holding a Milean battle banner and has a headful of pigtails, and there's a fully armed flying column marching across the flowery meadow. I skipped the graycoat on purpose, but now I cautiously peek at a sliver of him. His eyes have been x-ed out too, and there are three sturdy Milean arrows lodged through his head. Flowers sprout along the length of his bayonet, making it a bouquet, and each of his combat medals has been turned into a tiny skull. The battlefield behind him is full of Mileans in silhouette with fists and weapons raised in victory.

This is clearly not the same primer I had this morning.

I hold my posture carefully. Sab says someone is always listening, and if I give away that anything's amiss with my book, it will be taken and destroyed, and I could very well be blamed. Instead I turn the pages like I'm studying. Each picture has been altered, and every last one could easily get a girl brought before the inquisitors on a sedition charge.

There's someone at Forswelt like me. Someone else who has no plans to comply and obey. I grip my chair to keep from crowing with joy. Whoever she is, she's ungovernable too. I am not alone.

If she's here now, I have to find her. Together we'll form our own band of thirty, just like Everard Talshine, and even with our unbound hair and silly costumes, we'll still be worthy of our names. One by one, the other girls will join us. They will feel Milean again, and together we'll survive this place.

If she's already gone, at the very least I'll know it's possible to leave here a Milean. But that means it's up to me to make these girls understand what's at stake. Small acts of resistance are still acts of resistance, and in a place like this, they're the difference between staying Milean or ending up New Wealdan. All these girls have to do is follow my lead.

When it's time to put the books away, I linger till the others have gone and I can slide in my new favorite primer at the very end. I also nudge it so its spine is not quite even with the rest. If I have to sit through this class every other day, I want this primer each time, and I never want it discovered by a knuckle-under or an informer.

Dinner is more sandwiches, but this time I get half a bowl of meat chowder with a distinctly vegetable broth. Afterward, we're given free time, which isn't technically free because we're required to be there and we're separated into rooms by rank. I get a peek at the first-rank room as I walk past, and there are tables where you can play games or do handicrafts. There are trays of cut carrots and celery at the back. I can smell them from the doorway.

"Keep walking," says a novice standing watch in the hall, and she glares at me with her demerit pad in her hand till I'm well past.

The fourth-rank room has no tables, no games, no snacks. There are two ramshackle wooden chairs and a handful of grimy books piled haphazardly in a corner. The other fourth-rank girls are mostly straight from lower school. Babies, really, who should be playing hide-and-seek or marbles or kickball. None of them seems particularly talkative, and I'm wrung out from a gutful of bread and knowing I've loaded down my chambermates with more demerits in one day than they probably got all month. I spend the evening paging through each of the books. Some of them have pictures, but none have additions by my new mystery artist friend. I draw them in with my finger, line for line, like I remember from the primer. Just because no one else can see them doesn't mean I can't.

That primer might be the only thing my friend ever drew in. It might be my only clue to finding out who she is.

At bedtime, we're dismissed by rank to return to our chambers. The room is dim, lit faintly by a single gaslight wall sconce, and my chambermates are busying themselves with small woven baskets holding toothbrushes, washcloths, and combs. Fee's kneeling by her trunk, and when she stands up, her hair catches the light and she looks so much like my ma in that instant that I garble out a sudden, shuddering sob.

Fee turns, winces a smile, then hooks her elbow into mine where I'm frozen in the doorway. "It's time to go to the wash station. Get your shower basket. I'll show you."

"I'm not even supposed to be here," I mumble, swiping at stupid, pointless tears, because my ma wanted me to stay free and I am definitely not free.

"Sure you are. We all are." Fee opens my trunk, pulls out a basket identical to hers, and tucks it into my hands. "The first night is the hardest. Everyone cries. You should too. Get it out of the way."

The first night *was* the hardest. My parents had been caught. There'd be a trial, but there was no question what the verdict would be. The distracted Crown-appointed defense lawyer told me I'd be kept in the detention center and not in the guardhouse with the criminals, so I wouldn't be allowed to see my ma and da except in the courtroom. On that first night, I was curled up on a cot in my plain, cold room, trembling and worried and homesick already, when a blank-eyed Wealdan matron appeared in the door-way, told me it was bedtime, and cut the gaslight. Bedtime, and my da wouldn't be coming to kiss my forehead. My ma wouldn't tuck my blankets into my hammock and absently nudge it into motion like I was still small. I fought it down and fought it down, but then I broke and cried so deep and wrenching that my stomach hurt for hours afterward. No matter how loud I sobbed, no one came to see if I was all right.

No one ever will again.

"I can't cry. I can't. Then they win. They didn't break my ma and da. They won't break me." Tears are stream-ing down my face, and I clutch the basket handle because I've got to hang on to something. "If I cry, I'll never be songworthy. Jasperine didn't cry. She shouted *more wood* from her own pyre even as inquisitors splashed her with kerosene."

Fee shifts close enough to put an arm around my shoul-der. Tal and Sab are gone, and it's just us in the chamber. "Everyone cries. Even Loe. She'll deny it, but she did. For days."

"Loe?" I grab at the distraction. "That was my cantor's name."

"Yeah, I imagine it was." Fee sighs and pulls away. "The nuns take such joy in making Loe be a cantor. One of her ancestors was Everard Talshine."

The first line of a song runs through my head: *Everard stood at the mountain pass, his good sword in his hand.*

His great-granddaughter is here. At Forswelt. Not transported to one of the penal colonies. Not sent to the workhouse on account of her ancestor, who led the very first flying column against the Wealdan advance and has no less than seventeen different songs about him.

If anyone at this school knows how to resist, it'll be Loe. Someone who would bleed the songs we've all been taught, if she were cut. Together we'll help these girls remember what it is to be Milean. It'll be a relief to finally meet someone wide awake.

DAY 9

TODAY IS VOCATIONAL TRAINING, AND FEE reminds me to put on the proper uniform. It's a dress identical to the school uniform, only there's a cloaklike panel of fabric that Fee says is meant to keep your hair pressed against your back and out of your work.

"It doesn't count as binding," she assures me, but it's close enough, so I cheerfully cram my hair under it and go to breakfast.

After the meal, all four ranks go down a series of corridors until we step through a big arched doorway and into a courtyard. For a long moment, all I can do is breathe. The air is crisp and fresh, there's a breeze on my face, and even the mud underfoot feels alive after the unnatural smoothness of concrete and wood.

There are not enough windows in school. Not enough places the sun can get in. I knew to expect this, but that's not the same as living with it.

The courtyard door is secured by those same big complicated locks. There'll be no escaping, even if I had somewhere to go. I edge near Fee and ask, "We don't do training here?"

"No. The Cur estate."

I blink. "As in General Hock Cur? Butcher of the Burning Days? Who led the Lynch Legion and had Hesperus Dawnside drawn and quartered?"

Fee flinches, but it's gone in an instant. "The same. Best not to think on it too much."

"What could we possibly learn at his *house*?"

"Vocational training helps us learn to be useful to the empire," Fee replies, and I fight down a growl, because plows are useful. Pipes that carry water indoors are useful. *Things* are useful.

Being useful to the descendants of war criminals is the last thing I want, but one day I'll be done with this place. If I can learn a trade or a skill that will keep me from the debt traps the Wealdans have set, I'll hold my nose and get through it.

We shuffle along in rank order behind nuns on horseback, up a road bordered with vast fenced fields crammed with wildflowers and the occasional grazing pony. The walk isn't long, and soon a grand house made of stone and windows appears in slivers over the horizon. The nuns steer us away from the long carriageway that leads up to a big, fancy front door. Instead we all go around to the back, where we're met by a weather-beaten Milean woman in a uniform much like mine, only with the Embattled Crown an egg-size badge over her heart instead of stamped big across the chest.

"Honoras," she says in a voice that's at once respectful and yet quivering with barely concealed disdain.

I grin. I can't help it. I crane my neck to get a better look at her. Classically Milean. Too young to be a grand. Too old to have been to national school. Probably my parents' age. Just old enough to be wrung out by tithes and debt and the cold hopelessness of wage slavery, but not young enough to benefit from any of the reforms.

One of the Lost Generation. I know hundreds of songs about them, too. Really, every generation's been lost since Cav Horn blundered his way onto our shores and decided Milea's rich farmland ought to belong to Wealdans like him.

The fourth-rank girls are directed to a table loaded with buckets, scrub brushes, rags, and cakes of brown soap. We're told to take one of each and follow the Milean lady into a huge stone kitchen. She opens a door, and behind it is a dim servants' corridor lit with sputtering gaslight. We creep along inside the wall like rats and emerge through a small, discreet door set into the paneling of Cur Hall's sprawling front entryway.

A nun is there waiting for us. "Fourth rank, scrub this floor. Make a line so no one ruins anyone else's work."

The entryway is twice as big as the croft I grew up in. The floor is marble and freezing, and the walls are made of rich cedar paneling carefully inlaid with tiny wolf heads in contrasting shades of oak and milkwood. Above, there's a light fixture with hundreds of tiny gaslight nozzles shaped like flowers. The marble under the fixture is sticky with stray drips of fuel.

I turn to the nun, confused. "This isn't vocational. It's not even training! This is just . . . cleaning. That we're doing for *free*."

"Get to it, 1076, or I'll give every girl in this work group a demerit."

Around the entryway, girls are kneeling and pulling their buckets close. I do likewise, slamming the brush into the bucket, whacking it against the floor, and grinding the bristles against the marble.

"Easy," mutters the girl on my right. "You'll take the sheen off and then we'll have to polish, too."

"My cantor said something about vocational training," I reply, "but this can't be what she meant. None of this is going to help once I leave school."

"What'd you think she meant? The arts and crafts guilds? University? The military?" The girl scrubs in tiny, precise circles without looking up. "Besides, what makes you think you get to decide where you go once you leave? Sometime after you turn seventeen by their calendar— they never tell you exactly when—you'll be sent to work in a factory or in a Wealdan household. *Graduation*, they call it. That's how beds open up in the chambers."

My scrub brush jars to a halt. Willa the brain-dead factory girl, with her room in the lodginghouse very much like a chamber at school. Her cheerful gratitude. Her devotion to the empire. "No. I'm not living like this forever. With the rules and the chambermates, doing what I'm told so Wealdans can have nice lives. No."

"If you're lucky, you'll be sent to a grand house like the Cur estate so at least there'll be company," the girl goes on. "If not, well, you'll work so hard, you'll be too tired to think much on anything."

I sit back on my heels, fighting for breath. It's not enough that I have to grow up here. This is only the beginning. This is going to be my whole *life*.

"If it makes you feel any better," the girl adds in a softer tone, "I hate scrubbing floors too."

It's not like I've never scrubbed a floor. I had worse chores on the homestead. I've never scrubbed someone else's floor, though. I've never scrubbed a *useless* floor, one that's simply here to look pretty and maybe get walked on at holidays and the odd dinner party.

It doesn't take years and years of *vocational training* to teach us to clean and polish and tidy and haul. It might take that long to train us to stop thinking about it, though. It might take that long to make us give up the idea that there could be any other future.

DAY 11

I KEEP MY HEAD DOWN. I WEAR MY STUPID dresses and itchy undershifts. Everyone tells me not to think about things too much. Not thinking must be how you survive here, but I can't help myself. It's all I can do, because not thinking is how I'll lose everything Milean in me and become New Wealdan. I won't even mean to. Sooner or later, wearing a gown won't seem so strange. Willa the factory girl will seem happier and less brain-dead every day. When a girl makes a fuss over sandwiches in the dining hall, I'll wonder what her problem is. Malliane will turn her back on me because I'm unworthy of sharing her name, but I won't even care because I'll be Kem.

I have to do something songworthy, and I have to do it soon.

I'm about to make my bed when I notice Tal and Sab and Fee stripping the sheets and blankets off theirs. Tal opens our chamber door, and there are four parcels of folded woolens and linens lined up neatly in the hall. The bundles are tight and tidy, almost pretty, and arranged so each of our numbers is visible under the bow. Similar parcels sit next to other doors down the corridor, and the laundry basket in the corner of the room is no longer piled with our dirty uniforms and stockings and underwear.

I flip the bundle over so I won't have to see those squiggles in Wealdan. I'm not a number, just like I'm not a meat pie.

"Clean clothes," Fee explains. "Sheets and blankets, too. Put on a school dress. We've got chapel today."

Missing chapel got you a stiff fine in morality court, so one of the first things Master Grenallan taught us was how to go away. Not with our feet, but in our minds. "They can make you be there," he'd tell us, "but they can't make you hear. They can't make you *listen*."

So I don't. I kneel on the floor stones of the chapel with the other fourth-rank girls and do my da's trick of mouthing nonsense words instead of the proper chant of obedience. Sister Gunnhild reads a sermon on the importance of accepting your place in life and doing what you're told without complaining, but it's nothing but donkey braying if you breathe through your nose loudly enough. I start paying attention again when Sister Gunnhild closes her book, because that's when the inquisitors back in Trelawney Crossing would unlock the chapel doors and let people leave.

Only instead of the usual *Be diligent in your labor and mindful in your behavior,* Sister Gunnhild leans forward and says, "Before you're dismissed, I have wonderful news to share. The viceroy of New Weald will be making an official appearance at our school!"

Wonderful news. I'd sooner shovel out every stable at the Cur estate for a month without seeing the inside of the wash station than look one single time at the Crown-appointed governor of what used to be Milea.

"He's coming to celebrate discovery season," Sister Gunnhild goes on. "The best part is, he'll be here on Expansion Day itself!"

Expansion Day is months from now. It's going to be hard enough to wear the Embattled Crown on the day Cav Horn stumbled ashore all those years ago and found Mileans too busy with their harvests to pay him and his band of freebooters much mind. Having the viceroy here— the brute who signed my parents' transportation order to the penal colony—is going to be unbearable.

"There's been talk among the nobility of late that the national school program is too costly and not working like it should," Sister Gunnhild says. "Some even argue that it shouldn't be run by nuns! But your emperor is confident that the reforms are eliminating the need for harsher means of maintaining order, as well as making it easier for you to become happy, productive subjects. We're going to prove to him—*and* the taxpayers—that his efforts on your behalf aren't being wasted." Sister Gunnhild actually smiles, and her cheeks look like they'll splinter. "Girls, it's all been decided. You'll be putting on a production for the viceroy!"

A murmur goes through the crowd. I sit up straighter. This had better not mean what I think it means.

"Each of you will have a part in our show. We'll need stagehands and costume makers and set painters, but the luckiest of you will be actors. We're also planning to invite the Curs and the Neres, and possibly even the lords of Rudd, so the nobility can see firsthand how far you've come."

Ugh, even worse. The descendants of war criminals will be in the audience, including the senile old goat who petitioned for the Meadowlands Improvement Act that *redistricted* the land under our homestead and allowed the Gaudes to evict my family nice and legal once we couldn't pay the fees. Never mind that it blatantly went against the Relief Act, which limits the amount of money landlords can demand for permission to live on and work a piece of ground.

"I imagine you girls are eager to know more," Sister Gunnhild says. "Your teachers will share the script with you tomorrow in class and help prepare you for auditions. Not everyone will get an acting role, but each of you must try out."

I hide a shudder. I can see it now—girls in frilly Wealdan gowns, acting out some ridiculous melodrama cranked out by a playwright who has so many Milean servants to look after his house and children that he has nothing better to do than come up with plays by the pound.

Wait a minute. The viceroy is the emperor's brother, and they usually spend Expansion Day smugly waving to crowds from the imperial box in the capital during the parades. This year he's coming to Forswelt because the nuns have gone to a lot of trouble to get him here.

So I'm going to audition for that play. I'm going to win the lead role, and I'll see that every girl in this school makes such a hash of this production that the nuns will look as ridiculous in front of the viceroy as I feel answering to my meat-pie name.

This is going to be the best Expansion Day ever.

DAY 12

"ALL RIGHT, DIMWITS, LISTEN UP." SISTER Chlotilde produces a fat stack of papers from her desk. "We've only got a few months before Expansion Day, and that means we're already behind on this production. Auditions will be in three days. Each of you will give a flawless recitation. I will decide if any of you are worthy of being onstage. There will be no messing around or complaining or foot dragging, or you will *wish* for the crop. Am I making myself perfectly clear?"

We all mumble, "Yes, honora." I can't help but glance at the bookshelf where my seditious primer lives. The only thing that makes class remotely bearable, and now it'll be months before I'll get to look at it again.

Still, it's for a good cause.

"Good. I'm rearranging the reading groups so there'll be no excuses when it's time to audition." Sister Chlotilde directs us into clusters, all the while cradling her stack of papers like they're rare and precious. I'm in a group with Fee, a girl with brown skin named Koa who chews her fingernails nonstop, and Nim, a pale, freckled girl who has hair so bright I'd think she was Wealdan if I didn't know better. I shift my chair away from her the smallest bit.

Once we're settled in our new seats, Sister Chlotilde gives a handful of papers to each advanced reader. When she's down to the last few sheets, she hugs them and grins. It's a real smile too, one she might give another nun or even a friend, and it brightens her like steel wool against a brass cookpot. "History. This is where the *real* stories are. Great men, battles, rescues, adventure! When I volunteered for the national schools, I thought I'd be teaching *this*. Not the baby-level reading everyone ought to know by the time they're privy-trained."

Our group's advanced reader is Fee, and she clears her throat and reads off the first page, "The winning of New Weald. How the fearless explorer Cav Horn discovered and settled an uncharted world, and how a new land was made great."

This is a joke. It has to be. Because Cav Horn was neither fearless nor an explorer, and there was no winning. Not for us. Not in the occupation and subjugation and annexation of Milea.

"For the rest of class today, advanced readers will read the script aloud for your groups," Sister Chlotilde says. "Get to know it. Get to *love* it, because it's going to be the most important thing in your life for the next few months. Especially if you're an actor."

Everyone has to try out. Every last girl at Forswelt, hundreds of us, will have a hand in this production about the occupation and subjugation and annexation of Milea at the point of a sword and the passing of acts and the pyre and the workhouse and the *national school*.

Fee sighs and flips the page. "'Scene one. Cav Horn is standing on the deck of his ship, the *Inevitable*. He shades his eyes with his hand as he looks at the shore. Cav: What a green and lovely place! The God of All must favor me and my homeland specially, to send me here to claim it for our glorious empress and the Crown of Weald.'"

"But he *didn't!*" I protest. "Cav and his freebooters claimed Milea for themselves and set about demanding tribute from the ancestors. That's in *every single song*. He had to change his tune in a hurry when he started getting beaten back by the flying columns. He had to *beg* the Crown for soldiers to come help him—"

Fee and Koa and Nim are looking at me like I've lost my mind. They have to know the songs, same as me. I shut my mouth and study the desk. My plan to ruin the play was perfect when it was going to be some silly melodrama. I don't even want to *listen* to these lines, much less say any of them out loud, much less do it well enough to repeat them in front of war criminals.

"'General Cur: We will name this land New Weald, after our homeland that we love and cherish.'"

After the homeland that chased him into exile for attempting to overthrow the empress because she turned down his marriage proposal.

Fee reads three whole pages of Cav Horn and Hock Cur talking about how the endless green lands will enrich them and their followers, and how deserving they are of this reward, before they spot some New Wealdans. "'General Cur: The people here are primitive and misguided. Look at their pathetic, tiny farms. Look how they don't even have a market to sell goods. All they do is trade. And worse—*share*. We will help them, though. Think how much happier they will be when they are given honest work and taught to value it.'"

"Are you sure that's what those papers say?" I try not to sound angry because this is Fee, who's been nothing but kind since my first day. "The nuns made it seem like the production would be some sort of . . . *story*."

"It's a story, all right," mutters Nim.

"Why would I lie?" Fee straightens in her chair. "Kem, I thought you understood how it is here. Please, just let me finish reading."

I grip the edge of the table. "No. I'm not doing this. I'm not even going to say this stuff for an audition. None of you can do it either. This is serious. You have to listen to me."

Koa shrugs and traces her finger on the table.

Fee ignores me and keeps reading. "'Cav Horn: They won't appreciate the benefits of civilization at first, but they don't know what's good for them. If you let a child decide what he wants for supper every night, he will ask for nothing but cake.'" She looks up. "'Both men laugh.'"

I reach across and grab for the script, but Fee wrenches it away and glares. "Knock it off, Kem. Stop trying to get everyone in trouble."

"I'm *not*! I'm trying to make you see what's going on here! Then maybe someone will be a proper Milean and do something songworthy instead of knuckling under all the time!"

Fee's jaw drops. "What are you talking about? This isn't knuckling under! This is survival! Do you think I like this? Do you think they do?" She gestures to Koa and Nim, but they're determinedly studying the table. Then Fee rolls her eyes at Nim and adds, "Well, maybe *she* does."

"Don't drag me into this." Nim lifts her chin, and she has to be Wealdan but she can't be, because no Wealdan girl could do something so terrible that she'd be made to go to national school with Mileans and sleep on the same sheets and touch the same faucet knobs as us.

"I just want to get this over with," Koa mutters around what's left of her thumbnail.

All they've got to do is *listen* to me. My parents did the unthinkable—they not only attempted acts of industrial sabotage, but they were more successful than even the Crown wanted to let on. They watched more than one landlord burn to death through melting glass. I'm the most songworthy person in the room right now. That's not saying much, but at least it's something.

"Mess up your audition, then!" I whisper-shout. "Do *something!*"

Nim turns to Fee and says, "Better read. Not that I'm excited to hear it, but Sister Chlotilde's coming this way, and I really don't need more demerits."

I lean back in my chair, as far from her as I can get, and fold my arms tight. "Whatever. Knuckle-unders. Read, read, read. Wouldn't want to get in the way of all that compliance."

Fee narrows her eyes and finds her place in the script. Everard is *some petty criminal who cared nothing for the lives of his innocent children,* and Jasperine isn't mentioned at all. She is *one of the malcontents who engage in acts of brutality and violence* when most New Wealdans are grateful for Cav Horn and Hock Cur gallantly and decisively ensuring peace and laying the groundwork for a successful and productive society. These New Wealdans want no part of an ignorant, superstitious past, and they are eager to hear of the new wonders their saviors have brought for them to enjoy. Provinces are settled district by district. Inquisitors arrive and guide New Wealdans toward the holy truth. Land is redistricted to ensure that it's managed well and put to proper use. Acts are passed to maintain law and order. The Crown rewards brave men like Cav Horn and Hock

Cur, who brought such valuable resources into the empire, with estates befitting their new station.

Sister Chlotilde appears over Fee's shoulder. "Which part are you on?"

"The Wealdan ministers are, ah, recalibrating the labor force," Fee says to the script.

Evicting the Lost Generation from land their ancestors had farmed since Milea appeared out of the mists and forcing them to beg the Wealdans to let them work their own fields and pay for the privilege. While mourning the loss of their parents—the grands—to the workhouses.

"Ohhhh, that part is fascinating." Sister Chlotilde glances around our table like we're all choosing teams for hide-and-seek. "Are any of you thinking of trying out for the role of Cav Horn? You have promise, 13."

"Me?" Nim bares her teeth into a smile. "I'm not sure, honora. I'll think about it."

"That's what everyone keeps saying. All you girls." Sister Chlotilde's tone sharpens. "In fact, none of you seem exactly appreciative of this opportunity that we have put a lot of time and effort into securing for you. Let me tell you dimwits something. You will improve your attitudes, because you will not embarrass this school in front of the viceroy. All of us need this play to be an unqualified success."

The nun flourishes her crop, menacing, and Fee catches my eye. I hate to admit it, but she's right. Refusing to audition is a very bad idea.

"With any luck at all, some history will make its way into your brain meat. Maybe then you'll understand a little about the past and appreciate the viceroy's visit and what it means for the national school policy. The reforms you benefit from every day." Sister Chlotilde storms back to her desk, shaking her head and growling the whole way.

Fee finally gets to the last page. "'Narrator: So today, Expansion Day, we remember the struggle and sacrifice of those first explorers who brought together New Weald with the homeland, without whom our empire would not be nearly as great as it is now.'"

At the front of the room, Sister Chlotilde calls, "If your group finishes early, start memorizing a passage for your audition. Make sure it's at least ten lines long or there'll be consequences."

Across the table, Fee opens the script randomly to the middle and slides it so Koa can look too. They're going to comply. Reluctantly, maybe, but soon enough this sting will fade till it's simply one of many. This can't be where I leave it. If we're stuck doing a production and it's got to be a history production, maybe Sister Chlotilde would consider a few additions. She was downright pleasant today at just a mention of the past. It's possible she's never heard different stories.

A production about what really happened during the invasion might be tolerable. In fact, I wouldn't mind playing Jasperine. The nuns likely wouldn't let me have a rifle, even a pretend one, but I could settle for just giving her speech from the pyre, since I would be honoring her name and remembering her deeds, just like a schoolmaster making a song. I have to at least try. The worst thing that could happen is I'll get a demerit or two. At best I can make complying with this a little less awful for everyone.

After lunch, as the groups are gathering again with their scripts, I approach Sister Chlotilde at her desk. She looks calmer now, like a nice big meal put her in a better mood, and she peers up at me. "What is it?"

"I thought maybe we could change a few things in the script."

Sister Chlotilde frowns. "Like what?"

"There are lots of people missing," I reply, "like Jas—"

"The whole point of the production is to celebrate Expansion Day," Sister Chlotilde cuts in. "A day when we honor our history and how our great land was born. It would be inappropriate to glorify terrorists who used violence to advance their agenda, don't you think?"

Cav Horn hanging Everard's children one by one to bring him out of the greenwood sure sounds like a terrorist using violence to advance his agenda, but I know enough songs to make other suggestions. "All right. Then what about—?"

"The production script has been reviewed by the empire's foremost historians. We've gone to a lot of trouble to make it historically accurate. This is for the viceroy, after all. We didn't just slap it together." Sister Chlotilde narrows her eyes and I edge a step back. "It's important to show the past as it really was."

"But—"

"So go back to your seat and join your group," she goes on. "Since you're so interested in the production, you'll be auditioning with a passage from Johan Rule. The one where he warns the unfaithful of the consequences of heresy."

Johan Rule, who brought the Nameless God to Milea in the same ship as the first graycoats. Who dragged those massive anchor chains onto the beach and heated up the links one by one for the ancestors who had no plans to give up their souls to him or anyone.

Back at the table, Fee is reading the script again while Nim and Koa dutifully listen. I turn my face in their direction in case Sister Chlotilde is watching, but listening to a Milean voice say these things is filling my belly with poison. Not everyone resisted as Milea fell. Some people just learned to speak Wealdan. They mourned the loss of their name-kin but didn't rebuild the shrines. They kept their heads down and paid tithes and stayed clear of inquisitors. But if you were Everard and lost your hand at that icy pass, if you were Jasperine shouting *more wood* even as the flames from your pyre shot up like a curtain, all the kids in conquered Milea would know your name and sing your deeds and remember you with every word and note.

The moment the Wealdans realized this and began

disappearing people—quietly, anonymously, and without a trace—that was when Milea really fell. That was the day girls like me lost whatever power we might have had.

It's one thing to lose something. Another thing entirely to give it up. I'm not going to let these girls give up. One way or another, we are going to ruin this play. There can't be a girl in Forswelt who wants to put on a Cav Horn costume and talk about how deserving he was of a sprawling estate made up of stolen land. We just won't do it. We won't make costumes. We won't learn our lines. They can't punish all of us.

I won't get a better opportunity to be songworthy. I'm not about to let it pass me by.

DAY 15

IT'S AUDITION DAY. I EVEN VOLUNTEER TO GO first. Girls won't know how to resist unless I show them. I bumble and stammer. I say *uhhhh* a lot. I leave out a whole line about Johan Rule's fortitude and then pretend to remember and add it at the end, where it makes no sense. I shuffle my feet and let my attention wander instead of looking at the audience. By the end, half the class looks horrified and the other half is trying not to grin.

I'm assigned to set construction without much fanfare.

One by one, the rest of the class recites their passages. None of them mess up on purpose like I showed them. Some girls are nervous and stuttery, but they're obviously trying. Fee says her lines in a clear, boring monotone, staring straight ahead like a cantor giving the rules.

I fist up both hands under my desk. I am still alone.

Nim's audition isn't much better than mine, but Sister Chlotilde tells her she'll be playing Cav Horn, like it's already been decided. "It's the most important role in the whole play, and you're the only one who looks the part. Being chosen is the biggest honor. Massive. So don't foul it up."

Nim gurgles and presses a hand to her mouth like she's going to vomit. I barely know her, but as I head out of class with the other girls who were given nonacting roles, I silently wish her luck getting through it. I don't even like thinking about Cav Horn. Pretending to be him day after day—ugh, gives me the shudders.

There are about two dozen girls who will be making the stage, and the nun in charge of the construction is called Sister Gerta. She has a warm, round face, and hands that look like they've never held a hammer. Once all the girls assigned to do the work have gathered in her classroom, she leads us into a hallway I recognize from my first day here. The one that leads to the front door. She opens those complicated locks and shoos us into the grassy courtyard with only that tall iron fence across the lawn between us and home.

For a long moment, I squint at the low hills in the distance. My homestead is under two feet of horse manure by now, but I still have to make myself turn away.

The stage will stand a stone's throw from the big front door. There are a series of stakes pounded into the ground, with string running between them to mark where we'll build. Already there are several piles of logs arranged under tarps, along with crates of metal fasteners and braces and brackets. It's sunny and the wind smells like clover, and I have to blink back tears because I'm outside and it's the closest to home I'm likely to ever feel again.

Our first task is to cut the logs into boards, and I'm paired on a saw with a girl named Jey who can't hear. She speaks with her hands and does a bit of lip-reading like several kids did back in Trelawney Crossing. Sign language comes back to me right away, and I ask, *How's it going?*

Jey nods at Sister Gerta, who is sitting on a blanket under a parasol with a glass of ginger ale while the girls on set construction pick over saws and mallets, and she signs, *I'm outside, for a change. Also, I didn't even have to audition. Half the nuns don't have the patience to say more to me than they have to, and the other half can't understand a word I say.* She makes a sound-squiggle gesture near her mouth and rolls her eyes in an overdone way, and I smirk extra hard because after the disappointment of the other girls' auditions this morning, after smiling resignedly day after day at my chambermates, who just want to get along, I might have found someone as ungovernable as me.

Sawing is heavy, tiring work, but familiar; if you can run a plow, you can pull a saw. It's satisfying in a way sitting in a classroom isn't, and the sharp, fresh smell of sawdust makes me think of my da in his workshop, planing tall staves to trellis the pea crop or short ones to mark rows of radishes and carrots in our garden.

Tears come quick and jarring, and I blink hard. The idea to break machines was my da's. He actually grinned in our kitchen, a crowbar in his big hands, when he learned that the emperor had declared the Defense of Progress Act, which made the destruction of any machine a capital crime, the same as killing a person.

"The magistrates told me the Crown won't hear my petition against the new land dues they say we owe. It won't hear *any* Milean petitions that have to do with land." My da palmed his crowbar and I nodded, even though my parents had only twenty days to come up with those dues or else we'd lose our homestead and have to bind ourselves to a factory owner in exchange for room and board. "But apparently the Crown *will* hear Milean petitions if they're presented with the right amount of sledgehammering and kerosene and nobles squawking about lost profits. If this is how we have to petition, so be it."

The saw I'm holding is clever, clearly factory made, and there's a shiny metal screw fastening the handle to the blade. When Sister Gerta announces a water break and Jey heads over to the buckets and dippers, I sneak a screwdriver out of an unattended toolbox. I shake my hair till it hangs over my shoulder in an annoying damp curtain, then use it as a shield as I try to remove the saw handle.

Loom by loom, thresher by thresher, my parents left machines in pieces and burned down the sheds that housed them. My ma was the one who decided to start setting manor houses ablaze. She didn't care what the emperor would hear. "Land and rights or fire," my ma would sing under her breath to the same tune as "The Lament for Jasperine Vesley," and that scared me a little at the same time as it made me proud, because I knew what happened to Jasperine, but I also knew every one of the songworthy acts she did while she was alive.

Besides, only schoolmasters could make new songs, and my ma was an artisan and a farmer. She was by no means a schoolmaster.

The screw is halfway out of its hole, enough that I can turn it with my fingers. Likely this saw was made by some Milean in a factory somewhere who was nothing like brain-dead Willa and didn't care whether it held together or not.

A harsh shake to my shoulder. Jey's eyes are big. *What are you doing?*

This saw seems to be coming apart. Here. I toss her the screwdriver. *Do your end.*

Jey shakes her head and hands the tool back, gesturing

for me to fix the saw while glancing uneasily at Sister Gerta.

You want to do the production? I don't. If there's no stage, there can't be a production. No tools, no stage. When Jey just stands there shaking her head, it's too much and I fling the saw down with a bitten-down screech. *All right. Fine. I'm the only one. Somehow. All of you are complying. You're knuckling under. No one here but me is songworthy. Not that we can sing or anything. All of you should be ashamed to call yourself Mileans. But wait. You aren't. You're New Wealdans. A true Milean would have taken this tool from me. She would have started dismantling her saw. She would—*

Who are you to tell me what a true Milean would do? Jey asks, her motions sharp and angry.

Well— I make an awkward gesture that's nowhere near signing. *I know a lot of songs. I know the songworthy thing to do. And I don't see anyone here doing it!*

I know those stories too, Jey replies. *They're about joining a fight even though it's going to cost you something, maybe everything. They're about seeing something through, even when you know you can't win. They're about trying to preserve everyone's lives and homes and rights, not just your own. None of the songs are about putting yourself at risk when there's nothing to be gained. None of them are about blindly doing as you're told, no matter who's doing the telling.*

Jey grips her handle and hauls the saw back, then shoves it forward. The blade shifts and catches in the wood without someone at my end to steady it. She grinds it back

R IS FOR REBEL

and forth a few more times before pausing deliberately and meeting my eyes steady on.

Fine. If she's going to be this way, fine. Jasperine worked alone too. There are plenty of songs about Jasperine. Plenty. I pick up the stupid screwdriver and tighten the blade back in. Then I throw the tool back at the toolbox, grab my saw handle, and pull.

❁ 83 ❁

DAY 23

WHEN WE ARRIVE AT THE CUR ESTATE FOR vocational training, I'm pulled out of line and sent to stand under a tree with a number of other girls. Cantor Loe is one of them, and close up she's taller than I thought, and older than me too. I edge near her, but then I don't know what to say. She likely won't appreciate being reminded she was my cantor, and it would be ridiculous and awkward to introduce myself out of the blue. Just bringing up her ancestor's name will get us demerits, and that's the only thing that really links us. I'm still casting about when a nun leads us through the kitchen and along servants' corridors till we emerge in a long hallway lined with hundreds of portraits.

"You've been chosen for this task because you're the tall-est girls in this work group," the nun says. "Each of these portraits must be dusted. You are to touch only the frames, and only with the special cloths Novice Lilac is handing out. Do you understand?"

She says it like she expects us to have lots of questions and looks mildly surprised when we don't, so she directs each of us to a painting. The one I'm facing is a man in leather armor standing over a pile of corpses that have top-knots coming undone and pigtails trailing everywhere. He's holding a pole with a banner floating majestically from it, and behind him is the low bank of hills I recognize from the day I first got here, in the distance beyond Forswelt.

"I think I'd rather scrub chamber pots," I mutter. "At least the view is nicer."

Loe almost smiles as she dusts the picture next to mine.

It would be songworthy to poke my finger in the corner of this painting and rip it down and across. Separate this butcher's head from his body like he did to the Mileans who used to farm the land under my feet. I don't know who this man is. He's not Cav Horn or Hock Cur—I've seen enough woodcuts of those two to know them on sight—but I suddenly want to know, because maybe someone on the Roll of Honor took him down. It would be something to know that he died at the hands of a Milean and didn't live long enough to become convinced he had a right to the land he plundered.

There's a small brass tag at the bottom of the frame. I trace the cleaning cloth over the engraved letters, but they mean nothing to me. In class I focus on the pictures in the primer, trying to find a hidden message from my mystery friend that will help me work out who she is, so I still belong in a reading group all my own. Unwilling readers, maybe.

"Don't bother." Loe shakes dust out of her cloth.

"What?"

"You can't read it. It's complex." My confusion must be obvious, because Loe goes on, "We're taught to read simple Wealdan. That way, we can read road signs and factory machine settings and recipes and those special newspapers they make for us, telling us how great the empire is and how we should devote ourselves to it. Things we need to do the jobs they give us. Complex Wealdan is for literature and politics and law and holy texts. Tags at the bottom of paintings. We are definitely not taught those things."

There's a tone to *definitely* that makes me go still. Maybe I'm only hearing resistance in other people because I don't want to be alone with it. One of these times, though, my hopes are going to get crushed and stay crushed. I can barely look Jey in the eye now. But Loe smiles at me with a shadow of smirkiness, and all at once it makes sense.

Loe is the mystery artist. My secret friend.

No way would the great-granddaughter of Everard Talshine be complying without a whisper of resistance. She's figured out the secrets to surviving here. Things only a girl who's a part of the songs would know. Whatever she's doing is so far beneath the nuns' notice that she's even first rank, which means all the vegetables she can eat and the easiest jobs at vocational training. I have to know what those secrets are. I likely won't get another chance to ask. Not where there's no one close to overhear and inform.

"The topknots are wrong. In the painting." I gesture with the dusting cloth. "Did you notice?"

"I doubt the artist had ever seen Mileans," Loe replies. "The general probably described them for him. Or he read an account in one of the chronicles."

"Or he heard someone singing the Roll of Honor," I whisper. "Here are the few who stood for Milea."

Loe's rag slows for a long, long moment. I wait. No one else has any interest in resisting, even when there's every reason all around us, every day. She will. She has to. It's all over the primer she made. It's in her blood that all but hums with songs.

"Careful," Loe finally says in a quiet voice. "None of us is supposed to know about the others. This is not for you. Koa should have kept her mouth shut."

"Koa? She's in my production group. What about her? What others?"

Loe blinks hard. Then she mutters a swear and turns deliberately back to her dusting.

The others. Koa has a grand or an ancestor on the Roll of Honor, same as Loe. Same as who knows how many girls I sit near in class and stand with in dinner lines. Master Grenallan swore kids like Loe and Koa lived quietly in villages across the province, hidden in plain sight, but it was one of the few things I doubted him on. Yet here they are, and of course none of these girls are supposed to know others like them exist. They are the last echoes of a time when Mileans stood together and resisted.

Loe glances over her arm. The nun is at the other end of the hall, shouting at a second-rank girl for getting polish on the wallpaper. "Look, machine breaking and arson aren't nothing, and I'm not about to cry for a few burned-up factory owners wearing noble robes, but your ma and da are still alive. No disrespect. Really. So it doesn't compare, does it?"

Their gray, skeletal faces. Their shorn and bleeding scalps. Their posture, how they slumped like it was already over.

"You meet," I whisper. "The girls who are—like you. There's more than one of you, and you meet in secret."

Koa found out somehow who my ma and da are. She thought enough of them to say something to the great-granddaughter of Everard Talshine.

"Please." Loe speaks to the floor. "Please just forget I said anything."

"I thought it'd be just the two of us, but of course there are more. When can I meet them? The . . . honor girls?"

"I never said we met." Loe has gone utterly calm. "Just that there were others."

"Well . . ." I flounder. "Then we *should* meet. We should—"

"There is no we." Loe shakes her head, but kindly, like she's explaining to a tiny kid why she can't fly. "This is Forswelt, and it's everyone for herself. If you haven't figured that out yet, you're going to make things harder than they need to be."

"But that's why you made the primer!" I protest. "So anyone who thought to resist would know she wasn't alone!"

Loe frowns like she's trying to put something complicated into words, but then she tips her head meaningfully at the nun strolling back up the hallway, checking frames as she goes. Loe and I each turn to our dusting, but I keep trying to catch her eye so she can explain herself. She couldn't have altered that book and left it in the open without expecting girls to figure it out. The nun approves of my cleaning job and tells me to move to the next painting, but Loe is moved in the opposite direction, and she polishes her next frame with careful, graceful motions, without even a glance my way.

It's so unfair. Sure, my ma and da might not have single-handedly held off the Wealdan advance like Everard

Talshine, but they ruined enough machines to give Mileans a break from the most degrading part of their work, and they proved the Wealdan nobility in their fancy houses weren't as insulated from the consequences of their actions as they thought. When our valley was redistricted, our neighbors wept, then raged, then bound themselves to factory owners one by one.

My ma and da resisted.

Not me, though. Not here. I just complied. Still not a whisper of resistance despite all my big talk, and now I'm in front of a portrait of Maude Cur, the current lady of the estate, and she's wearing her military graycoat and regarding me with a disdain that makes me look at her feet immediately. Only you can't see her feet in the painting. Just the brass tag I'll never be taught to read.

Milea took years to become governable. I fell in three lousy weeks. I haven't lost a hand. I haven't had to shout *more wood*. I'm keeping my head down and avoiding demerits instead of standing up for myself. I'm sawing boards to make a stage where Milean girls will act out the conquest of their homeland for the amusement of its governor. All I've done is talk, and no one's even listening, because we're all learning deference and compliance and a proper work ethic here, away from the misleading influence of our ignorant parents. I'm becoming governable. Just like the Education Act would have us be.

Malliane must already be turning her back on me. She

won't claim me as her name-kin, and she's right not to. Not if this is how I'm ending up.

As we're leaving the Cur estate in the late afternoon, we're held up in the kitchen while the grooms bring the nuns' horses around from the stables. The ceilings are high and elegant, the cabinets all shine with dark wood, and the maple countertops gleam with hours of Milean sweat and sore muscles and dulled-down thoughts of compliance. The counters are mostly bare and shining, but behind a big glass vase of cut flowers is a small palm-blade for removing leaves and trimming stems.

I grab that blade quick and subtle, seize a wisp of my hair, cut it right at the roots, and shove it in my uniform pocket. It's blasphemy—metal should never touch a Milean's hair—but there's no other way. I'm done helping the Wealdans make me into Kem. I'm done ignoring the things that make me who I am because it's easier.

That night, during free time, I ask to go to the privy, and there on the seat I weave the wisp of hair in Malliane's pattern and tie it at both ends with a ravel of loose wool from my gown. The trail of braid lies on my lap, winding and chaotic. My heart pounds so hard it hurts, because all I can think about is the *shink-shink* of the shears from that first day at Forswelt, but then the old wash of warmth comes over me too, like Malliane herself is nodding approval from her place among the ancestors.

I've bound my hair.

I coil the plait and tuck it deep into my pocket. It will do its work even if no one knows it's there but me and my name-kin. Malliane will still recognize me as one of hers. She has to. Otherwise I'm not Milean anymore, and none of this matters at all.

DAY 28

EVEN THOUGH WE'RE BUSY WITH THE PLAY,
Sister Gunnhild insists we have two days of instruction
per week. She says it's to keep us from backsliding on our
learning, but it's likely so the school stays in compliance
with the Education Act. Master Grenallan made sure each
of us could recite the provisions of that act so we'd know
our rights. "They're counting on your ignorance," he'd say.
"They'll try to replace what you know is true with what
they want you to believe is true."

The worst day outside is better than the best day inside,
but if I'm in class, at least I can enjoy the seditious primer.
When we file in after breakfast, Sister Chlotilde waves us
impatiently toward the window, growling, "Find a book.
Hurry up."

I get to the bookcase at the same time Jey is reaching for the seditious primer. My heart lurches and I grab that book and pull, hissing something incoherent, but she doesn't let go. The book seesaws between us once—twice—before it slips out of my sweaty grip and I stumble backward.

Jey stares at me openmouthed before shoving the primer into her armpit and saying, *What are you doing? What's wrong with you?*

"Nothing. Nothing." I'm so upset I forget to sign, but Jey's confusion snaps me back. *Just . . . that primer is mine.*

Nothing here is ours. Jey rolls her eyes. *You don't have to be a jerk about it.*

No. I mean . . . I grab a primer at random off the shelf. *Take this one. Trade me.*

"What's going on over there?" Sister Chlotilde lowers her newspaper. "Do you really want me to get up?"

I yank the seditious primer out from under Jey's arm and shove the ordinary one at her. She scoffs, loud, like she can't believe what a pain I'm being. But she's not heading for her seat. She's not going to let this go.

Sister Chlotilde slams her paper on her desk, heaves her chair back, and approaches us slow and ominous. Jey and I both go still like you do when an inquisitor calls, *halt.*

"Apparently there's a problem over here." Sister Chlotilde surveys Jey and me. "Or maybe this is stupid girls being stupid. Maybe both of you want to take a demerit for disrupting my class and hope none of your dimwit class-mates are too upset that every group will be reading aloud today because of you."

The whole class groans. Jey glares at me long and poisonous. Sister Chlotilde only signs when the mood strikes her, but Jey knows as well as I do that responding in any way will be considered talking back, and it's a sure way to multiple demerits and possibly solo read-alouds in front of the whole class and definitely the crop across something soft and fleshy.

So I say, "Yes, honora," because it's the only thing that might get me clear of this with my primer in hand, even if I'll get another chewing-out about how ignorant I am for not knowing all the letters yet.

Jey bows her head, which must be good enough for Sister Chlotilde, because she scowls at both of us and moves toward her desk. Once her back is turned, Jey signs something I'm pretty sure is a string of swears, which ordinarily would make me grin and give her a secret thumbs-up, and now that I have my primer back, it's easy to be forgiving. Only Sister Chlotilde doesn't sit down and start class. She shuffles papers till she finds her demerit pad and a pen. I muffle a groan because my chambermates are not going to be happy about another demerit, and that's when Jey lunges—

—catches the primer by its cover—

—and pulls. The primer comes loose from my hand

and hits the floor. The binding cracks and pages scatter at our feet.

The baby and his Milean pigtails.

The flying column in the field.

The graycoat and his x-ed-out eyes and his skullified combat medals.

I suck in a squeaky breath. Jey's eyes go huge, and she clutches her ordinary primer and flees back to her table.

"Careless idiots." Sister Chlotilde is scribbling on her demerit pad while stomping toward me. "Can't even be trusted to take care of school property. Honestly, I don't know . . . how . . ." Her gaze drops to the floor planks. Her arm goes limp and carries her demerit pad lifelessly to her side. Then she fixes me with the kind of look I never want to see on a Wealdan's face, but her voice is oddly calm when she says, "What is the meaning of this?"

I lick my lips. Resistance is the meaning of this. Staying Milean in whatever way we can. I look her in the feet. It's all I can think to do.

"Pick them up. The pages. Get on the floor and *pick them up.*"

I do. I drop like a stone. My hands tremble as I sweep the stray papers into a pile and tuck them into the two halves of the cover. Loe will never forgive me. Her primer will be sent straight to the incinerator and it's my fault. My chambermates will end up demoted to fourth rank. Or worse. All my stupid, *stupid* fault.

I hand what's left of the seditious primer to Sister Chlotilde, and she takes her time flipping through the pages that are still bound. Shaking her head, slow and murderous. Then she closes the cover like she's lowering the lid on a coffin. "Did you deface this book, 1076?"

The way she says it tells me it doesn't matter how I respond. The punishment's going to be the same, and it's going to be bad. So I might as well go out like a true Milean. I might as well do the songworthy thing.

Fee catches my eye. She mouths the word *beg*. Tal is studying the table, her cheeks red, and Sab is openly, silently panicking.

I'm not begging. My ma and da didn't. Jasperine and Everard didn't. My chambermates might not want to be songworthy, but today they're going to have to be. I have to show them how it's done. They've been so long without the songs that they've forgotten how.

So I stand up straight. Chin raised, eyes defiant, fierce and true and Milean, and I nod to Sister Chlotilde. I hope I look the part, because my heart is racing and I am an instant from collapsing on the classroom floor.

Sister Chlotilde shakes her head, disgusted, like she knew it all along. "1076, face the room. Your chambermates, too. On your feet. Chamber 47 receives fifty demerits each for insulting the dignity of the Crown."

The room pulls in a breath, but all I hear is Fee's sharp gasp and Sab's muffled screech.

My chambermates will resist now that they know what to do. Now that there's nothing else left to them. We'll hold together like a flying column. No Milean would let this opportunity pass her by. I didn't mean for this to happen, but now that it's happening, they might as well rise to the occasion.

Only they're not. Sab is bawling, loud, like a baby when you take away a toy, and Tal and Fee both sniffle quietly into their hands. They look pitiful and weak and defeated, and it makes me angry, though at the same time I'm a heartbeat from crying too.

Sister Chlotilde herds the four of us into the hall, then shouts for novices. While she's waiting, she shoves us each against the wall and whips our scarves off our necks one by one. She flings them into a pile like they're filthy. I look straight ahead. I'm shaking all over. My chambermates had a chance to be like Jasperine and Everard, and they spent it sobbing and cringing. They would have had me beg.

They're not worthy of their names, whatever those might be. None of them are.

Novices appear, and they march Tal and Fee and Sab away to their correctional vocational sentences. There's no rank order this time. We're all as far down on the punishment scale as a girl can get and still be in school. Soon enough, Novice Peony is hustling me along corridors that get darker and hotter and damper as we go. I give up struggling and let myself be led. The songs are running through my head now. So many are about how to die well. How to be bold and true, how to meet your fate with a smile.

I clutch my uniform pocket and the plait curled at the bottom. Malliane is watching. I have to be like her. As much as I can, especially after my chambermates failed so spectacularly. My primer is gone. My former chambermates will hate me till they die. This plait and my namekin are what I have left now that I've been sent below.

At the bottom of a ramp, Novice Peony wrenches me to a stop and unlocks a door. We step into a cavernous room that's lined on all four walls with counters and long, deep sinks. It's bright with gaslight and blindingly, unmercifully hot. At each sink, a girl stands with her back to the room, wearing only her undershift and no stockings. Carts on wheels are stationed everywhere, and piles of wool and linen are heaped on the counters, acres and acres of it, gowns of every size and washrags and towels and stockings and bedsheets. Billows of steam rise from the sinks and pipes rattle overhead. There are buckets at each girl's feet, and standing water in divots and grids across the brickwork floor.

The laundry. I've been sent to the laundry.

"Prefect!" Novice Peony's voice echoes in the humid, clanging tomb, barely audible over the hiss of the steam and the jangling of dozens and dozens of hand-wringers and a low, mumbly chanting that seems to hang in the damp air.

A Milean girl comes over, wiping her hands on a towel. She's got topknot ribbons wound gracefully around her neck and along her arms, and her hair rolls away from her face in bouncy brown waves. Her face is ruddy-pink from the heat, and she looks so much like my friend Vallalia, who had to be sold into factory service when we were barely old enough for topknots, that I fight down a sudden choke in my throat.

This girl gets ribbons when no one else does. She's earned a privilege with compliance.

"New meat for you, Zoh. Insulted the dignity of the Crown." Novice Peony looses me roughly, and I splash into a puddle that soaks through my felt shoes and stockings in a warm, disgusting instant.

Zoh jerks her chin toward a sink and says, "Follow." She says it like she's a nun, and my heart sinks. Somehow knowing a girl like me is in charge of enforcing compliance is worse than being ordered around by Wealdans.

I grit my teeth. I scrub at stupid tears and do what I'm told. There's nothing like this in a song. Songs end in glory, not you standing in a steam pit with your hair shriveling into wet strings and your dress clinging to your back in a moist, clammy sheet.

Zoh approaches a red-cheeked girl working at one of the massive sinks and thumps her on the shoulder. "634.

You're promoted to ironing. Show 1076 how to wash, then report to the pressing room prefect for your new task set."

The girl nods and turns to me, but she waits for Zoh to leave before saying, "I'm Bet. You must be wrecked to be down here, whatever you did, but pay attention, all right?"

I mean to tell her my school name, but I choke because I did the songworthy thing and resisted and it got me nothing except three ex-friends and no one to remember my deeds and honor my memory.

"This is your station. You'll stand here every day washing till the work is done." Bet waves a hand over a sink divided into four parts, one of which has a scrubbing board poking out. "If you ruin clothing, you'll work off the cost, so be careful to only use as much bluing as you need."

I nod blearily. Like the workhouse. The *other* workhouse, the legal one.

"This is bluing." Bet leans down and pulls a covered metal pail from a shelf under the sink. "It's the cleaner we use. Never, *never* touch it with your hands or it'll burn you. Always use the measuring scoop—carefully. Bluing dissolves slow, so give it time and don't just add extra. Each section of the sink should be a different strength of bluing. Be sure to mix it right. Use the lines on the scoop. I'm away to the pressing room. Good luck."

There's a long wooden table next to the sink covered in sopping gowns, and at the end of it is a brown-skinned girl with curly black hair feeding clothing through a metal wringer that she cranks with her other hand. After she wrings out each dress or shift, she tosses it into one of those big carts on wheels stationed nearby.

"Hurry," the wringer girl says, but not in a mean way. More in an earnest way, like she's trying to help me. She points to the fill line near the top of the sink and gestures like I should turn on the tap. I do, and then she foot-nudges a full bucket toward me while still cranking the wringer handle. I add cold water from the bucket like I saw other girls doing, and the instant it's empty, a powder-pale, scurrying girl crouches to whisk the bucket away and replace it with a full one.

The bucket girl is halfway to her feet when she does a double take and mutters to the wringer girl, "Holy shrines, Gaddy, they're giving them shoes now!"

Gaddy hisses, and the bucket girl slaps a hand over her mouth and flitters away toward a cart piled high with buckets both full and empty. I'm parsing the name—Gaddy isn't any word in Wealdan that I know—when she cuts past me and turns off the faucet just as the water laps dangerously close to the sink rim.

I'm curious enough to try the other handle, but nothing happens. "Why isn't there a cold tap too?"

"The prefects turned off a water main to make more work for us," Gaddy replies patiently. "Now please just start washing or we're going to be here all night."

I station the washboard in the sink section with the

least amount of bluing, pick up a shift, and scrub it on the board. There are underpants, too, but washing someone else's underwear seems way too personal. When the shift looks clean, I swish it around in the rinse water, wring it out, then put it on the other counter. Gaddy grabs it, twists it hard so water drips into the bucket at her feet, feeds it though the metal wringer, then lays it flat in her cart. Then she looks at me expectantly, and I realize she wants me to scrub something else.

As I reach for another shift, a door opens and a pale girl with matted mousy hair stumbles in, straining to push a huge cart loaded with piles of dingy linen. She steers it toward my sink and methodically lifts armloads of dirty clothes onto the left-hand counter. The cart doesn't seem to have a bottom. After the clothes, there are rancid, nasty towels that smell like kitchen grease, and they've smeared all over some stockings that would have been a breeze to wash. Pretty soon, the counter is buried under a massive heap of laundry.

We're going to be here all night.

I turn back to my sink and wash with a will. I scrub and plunge, scrub and plunge. As fast as I can lay clean clothes on the right-hand counter, Gaddy squeezes out more water, cranks them through the wringer, and lays them in the cart. When the cart fills up, a different girl appears and wheels it away. The left-hand pile never gets lower. Everything I wash seems to sneak back into the heap filthier or greasier.

My uniform is drenched and I'm sweltering. Sweat and

wash water, it's all the same. Now I see why everyone has stripped down to their shifts, why they're going without shoes and stockings. I do likewise. I'm instantly more comfortable, even though my hair still sticks to my bare arms like a damp, stringy cloud and clings to my neck like a noose.

The door bangs open and the cart girl rolls in another heaping load. There are more uniforms and underwear, but also the towels we use in the wash station. It can't be evening already, but these towels are moldy and ripe enough that they could be from days ago, and I don't ask. I don't care. I just grapple them into the part of the sink with the most bluing.

Zoh is there whenever I start to buckle, and she whispers in my ear that failing to learn from my corrective vocational assignment means I'm ungovernable, and everyone knows what happens to girls who are ungovernable.

My hands get wrinkly, then raw. My back has fallen in and I can't feel my feet, but I've sunk into a rhythm. It keeps me from thinking too much about anything but soap and water and the cheap unbleached linen I would be happy if I never have to see again. I'm not thinking how songworthy acts in real life are nothing like they are in songs. I'm not thinking about the chambermates who I was sure would stand with me, who could have at least faced their own correctional sentences with a teaspoonful of whatever made Jasperine shout *more wood*. The only tiny turn of joy in all this is not having anything more to do with that stupid production for the stupid viceroy.

A door clunks open at the far end of the room, one I hadn't noticed, and this time the cart is buried under sheets of canvas caked with grease and massive tablecloths smeared with gobs of eggs and mustard and gristle, and somehow I turn the tap. I heave up the bucket. I drain and refill the rinse water when it's too full of bluing suds. I scrub and wince and squirm as blood from my cracked fingernails curls into it.

Ten more rags. Nine. Mop heads in a tangle. Not much longer. Then I can sleep.

I'm down to my last two rags when the access door opens and the cart girl bangs through. She looks worse than I feel—hands blistered, eyes reddened, face steam-blasted. Her cart is loaded with more tablecloths, and these are littered with cake crumbs, pudding smears, and tea stains. We never have fancy desserts, so this must be from the nuns' dining room.

The cart girl heads right for me.

"Wait, stop!" I protest, but she clangs the wretched thing against my counter even as I slide the last rag toward Gaddy for wringing. "I'm done. I'm going to bed. I can't . . ."

"Sorry." The cart girl's mutter is low and raspy, but sincere. The wooden counter disappears under more drapes and folds and stains as I stand there swaying on my feet.

"Well?" Zoh appears out of the steam, a mug of tea hooked

over one finger. "Better get to it. Your bed's under your sink when you're finished, but you're clearly not finished." She almost smiles. "Perhaps tomorrow you'll be faster."

Someone shakes my shoulder. A tremor of white-hot agony jolts down my arm, and even that only drags me a little awake. There's something wrong with my pillow. It feels like the bare dirty ground and smells like winter cloaks when you pull them out of storage in the fall.

"Hey. *Hey.* Wake up!"

Another jostle, another jolt of pain, and I am going to tell whoever this is what she can do with—

Wait. That was *Milean.* This girl is speaking an outlawed tongue without hesitation or fear.

I shift my elbow under me just as the voice is telling me not to sit up, and I crack my head against something hard and metal. Pipes. The pipes under a big trough sink in the laundry.

I'm not in my bed in chamber 47. Because I wouldn't— couldn't—let someone else look at the seditious primer. The primer I'd started calling *mine,* when if it was any-one's, it was Loe's.

"Tried to tell you," the voice whispers in Milean. "Roll out first. Then sit up. Keep it quiet."

I do. Blearily. The laundry is dark but for the row of small windows spaced around the top of the walls just below the ceiling and a swiff of orange light an arm's length from me. The girl kneeling there holds a dish of grease with a wick in it. Her face is softly lit from the smudge of flame she's holding in her two hands cupped together, like it's a baby bird or a grandma's ribbon or some other fragile, priceless thing.

"Come with me," she says, and that's when I realize the laundry is alive with the tiny sounds of people shifting in the dark. Another orange smudge lights up against the far wall, and shadows start forming into girls.

I haven't heard a word in Milean since that last night in the guardhouse with my ma and da. This can't be real. I'm dreaming, or I'm dead.

When I don't move, she smiles, open and kind. No trace of mocking or cruelty. The kind of greeting you'd get from a friend you haven't seen in ages, and I choke because it's been at least that long since I've seen a smile like that.

So I climb to my feet. I'm almost in tears, it hurts so bad to move. The girl grins bigger and sways into motion toward the ring of people against the far wall, hidden in the shadow where two big bronze counters fit together. She sits cross-legged in a gap in the circle and looks up at me expectantly. I sink down beside her, hissing and gasping with every tiny, painful movement. Gaddy is on my other side, and a few places down from her sits the bird-thin bucket girl who couldn't believe I was wearing shoes.

"I'm Dollinemell." The girl who brought me here says

it clear and precise, polishing every syllable, and the others say her name after her, low and murmury, like a chant. Then she hands the little homemade lamp to the cart girl, and she says her Milean name in a quiet but purposeful way. The others echo it, and it's eerily like the Roll of Honor.

They give their nicknames, too. Emmy for Dollinemell. Cara for Caramarienne, who pushes the cart. We may share ungovernable names, but we carry them in our own way. It takes my breath away how easily they open up, like we're cradle-friends meeting to climb trees or forage, the sun on our backs and leaves in our topknots. Like the Education Act does not reach us here in the laundry.

At last the lamp makes it around to me. I grip the dish and breathe, "Why? You don't know me nearly well enough to trust me. With your Milean names. With all this."

Emmy shrugs, but her smile is sad. "We can't gather like this without every girl in the laundry knowing. If we don't meet, there'll be nothing to look forward to and the laundry will end us. So you're a part of it, come what may. You want to inform on us? Zoh's room is just off the entrance. She gets one to herself. It's almost definitely your ticket back topside. Only do it now if you're going to do it. We'd rather see it coming."

I count quickly. Eleven girls, plus me. This is everyone in the laundry. No one is even looking at Zoh's door. Even after a day on their feet. Their hands as wrinkly and stiff as mine.

"Malliane," I murmur, and it's like getting a hug from my ma to be talking in Milean after so many months speaking nothing but Wealdan, at school but also at the detention center and the trial, my parents' lawyer sternly telling me not to even *think* a word in Milean in case it slipped out and reminded the judge how serious the charges already were. So I say it louder, in a quiet, sharp voice just above a whisper. "Malliane Pirine Vinnio Aurelia Hesperus, of Salix Homestead in Trelawney Crossing, Lavender Province, Milea."

Emmy grins. Not like she's grateful or even surprised. More like she knew all along what I would do and she's happy to have a piece of business out of the way. "Now. Who's got a report?"

Someone starts talking about the noise level and how well it's drowning out the novice chanting chapel prayers nonstop from the observation room, and another girl wants everyone to know that Zoh is filling the bluing containers very full and we should be extra careful. The shock of being startled awake is wearing off, and my eyelids are beginning to drag despite how bad my muscles are screaming from sitting on cold concrete. Hearing Milean again puts a dull, bittersweet ache at the back of my throat, but it fills cracks in me that have stood empty since that first night I fled the guardhouse, crying in the dark.

"Anything else? No other reports?" Emmy glances around the circle. "What's tonight's lesson? Aurelia?"

"I'd planned a talk on critical thinking and principles of logic, but since we have someone new"—Aurelia smiles at me—"and part of my name-kin to boot, I think we'll do a recitation."

"A recitation?" I jerk awake. "You mean the Roll of Honor?"

Aurelia nods. "Would you like to start? Or maybe not. You're crying. Maybe you'd like a moment to collect yourself?"

It's hitting me now, through the bone-weariness and the agony in even my tiniest muscles, what this is. Mileans meeting in secret like the flying columns did, hidden from an inquisitor who would have them torn up with the whip and sent to the workhouse. Reports of recent happenings and a lesson to be shared.

This is a hedge school.

"We can't," I say, and as girls frown, confused and hurt, I go on, "This can't be a hedge school. Not that I don't want it to be. I do. But there are no more schoolmasters, so there can't be any hedge school."

"We're all schoolmasters now," Gaddy replies, and the other girls nod solemnly, like it's something they say and hear often.

"But you *can't* be," I protest. "We've lost so much. We have to hold tight to everything that's left. Keep it just like it was."

Emmy shakes her head. "That's how you end up with

nothing. When you can't bring the best parts of the past with you into the future."

"There's not going to be a future," I mutter. "This place is already seeing to that. No one remembers the songs. Nobody else resists. Only me."

"How do you know?" Gaddy asks quietly. "Maybe they do, but not in the same way as you."

I shake my head. "They can't. Otherwise they'd *act* like it."

"Other people aren't wrong just because they don't agree with you," Emmy replies.

I know those stories too. I thought the worst of Jey, but she wasn't wrong. Not being able to hear music means she has to know the songs her own way, and it can't be easy. It matters to her, though, because she still holds them as tight as any one of us.

"You're not seeing it, then," Gaddy says to me, and she gestures around the orange-lit circle of girls with their wash-worn hands and matted, tangly hair. "How others resist. Maybe you're not even looking."

Master Grenallan's last apprentice was disappeared along with him, although a boy in Trelawney Crossing did find several of her pigtails scattered in the woods. It won't be long before little kids in lower school won't know what a schoolmaster is. They'll have never gone to hedge school. They won't even have one another. They'll be keeping their heads down and avoiding demerits instead of standing up for themselves, and they'll end up useful to the empire because they know nothing else to do. Not only will my tiny friends never know the songs, they won't even know songs existed. They will never resist because they'll never know they can—and should.

That's when Milea will have well and truly fallen.

I can't bring myself to say I'm a schoolmaster like Gaddy and Emmy can, but I can sit with these girls. I can recite the story of my name-kin. And for a few hours tonight, I can feel like home is just beyond the circle of candlelight in this dark place.

DAYS AND DAYS

I'M GETTING THE HANG OF THE LAUNDRY. It's not difficult. Just exhausting, and staying up half the night for hedge school doesn't help. But one morning I turn the hot tap and it spins free and only a tiny trickle of water comes out.

"Gaddy! This can't be right. Come look."

Gaddy steps over from the wringer and her eyes go wide. "Oh no. This is bad."

"Prefect!" I wave an arm till Zoh frowns at me. "Something's wrong with the faucet. What do we do?"

"I'm not interested in your excuses. You stand at your sink till the work is finished." Zoh scritches on her clipboard, shaking her head in overdone dismay. "Work ethic:

unsatisfactory. Behavior: confrontational. Look at all these boxes I have to check! A report like this will bring the nuns down for an inspection, 1076."

I twist the faucet harder, like that will help somehow. I've been in the laundry long enough to know we're beyond demerits, and a prefect's word alone is enough to get someone disappeared.

Gaddy starts pacing. "This happened another time. The clasp that holds the faucet to the pipe wore away. We had to take the whole sink apart. It was down for days and we had to wash what we could in buckets. You should have seen the piles of laundry that backed up. Once it was fixed, we had overnight shifts for two weeks till every last thing got clean."

Making it through the day is hard enough on nothing but sandwiches and the fear of too much attention from Zoh. If we have to work all night, there can't be any hedge school, and even though it still feels blasphemous to sit for lessons without a proper schoolmaster, just knowing it's happening keeps the laundry from ending me a little more each day.

Gaddy brightens. "Maybe I can clean and tighten the clasp. That might help."

"Let's hope so. I'm going to start washing with the water we have."

"You can't wash in cold water." Gaddy pushes the washboard out of my reach. "The bluing won't dissolve."

"All right," I say, but as soon as she's under the sink, I

gingerly pull out the metal container and sprinkle a scoop of pale crystals into the heavy-wash vat. They sink to the bottom, not fizzing like they should. I stab them with the stirring paddle and they seem to crumble, so I pour in a bucket of cold water. Even though there's clunking and cursing coming from under the sink, the hot water is still barely dribbling, and if I don't wash the greasy breakfast rags from the kitchen early, they'll slow up my whole line for the day. I toss them into the sink and poke them with the paddle, but they just float there. They don't hiss or steam or disintegrate like I was afraid they would. Maybe just the little bit of warm water trickling in is enough to make the bluing work properly. Zoh sees me standing helplessly in front of a half-full sink, then checks more boxes on her clipboard with big swings of her pencil. Then she smiles, slow and poisonous.

I dump a second bucket of cold water and slide the washboard into the vat. I reach into the water, grab the dirtiest towel, and scrub exactly twice before a wave of fiery agony shoots up my fingers and over my hands and toward my elbows. I shriek and whip my hands out and shriek again because they're turning a vivid purple and big shiny blisters the size of peach pits are following like a march of ants.

I am screaming and my hands and arms are blistering before my eyes and then they're being plunged into clean rinse water by two hands that aren't mine, two calloused brown hands with bitten-off nails that belong to Gaddy.

"You're all right. You're all right. Don't look. Leave them in the water. I'm going to get Zoh. Just stay here and *don't look.*"

The rinse water doesn't help. Not at all. I lean both elbows against the sink and grind out breath after sobbing, screeching breath till I'm sick down the front of my sweat-crusty undershift.

". . . pretty badly . . . infirmary . . ."

". . . tape her up . . . bone-stupid . . . got what she deserved if she can't follow simple instructions . . ."

I am on a low, teetery wooden stool. Cara is dipping frayed strips of linen in a clear gel, her cart a dark blur behind her. Gaddy is whispering, "This is going to hurt. Sorry."

Things hurt when they matter. That's what my da would say when we'd eat yet another meal of bog turnips stolen from fenced-off marshland because there was nothing else. He'd watch our neighbors shuffling behind the plow, weak and penniless and grainsick, and shake his head. Once I asked why he didn't make them come with him to *obtain* decent food and he said, "I can't decide for someone else when that last straw breaks. This doesn't hurt enough yet. They'll know when they get there."

Gaddy wraps the moistened strips around my burned forearms and fingers sure and steady, but it's agony. This is what it feels like to die by fire. I should be shouting *more wood* like Jasperine, but I can only grit my teeth and whimper and sob like the unsongworthy wreck I am.

"Done." Gaddy smiles like nothing is wrong, but the rest of her face is scared and angry and worried.

"Thank you," I murmur, and I want to hug her but I can barely lift my arms. I collapse to my knees so I can crawl onto my pallet and sleep for a year, but Gaddy catches my sleeve. She looks bellysick as she nods toward the sink. The water level is reaching the fill line, steam rising gently like it didn't just eat away my arm meat.

It takes me a moment. Everything is still on fire. "You . . . you mean I have to keep washing?"

Gaddy shifts uncomfortably. "The clasp just needed tightening. The tap's working a lot better now."

Cara's unloading the second cart of the morning. The left-hand table is so loaded down it's impossible to sort everything into piles. Zoh watches from her stool at her surveillance station.

There's a flush of red near my elbows where the bandages don't quite cover. I force my fingers to curl around a pair of underpants and push them into the light-wash vat. The hot water soaks my bandages in an instant and hits the blisters like acid. I pull in a hard breath and buckle against the sink, then recover. Straighten. Blink back tears. Start scrubbing.

I lie sweating and twitching on my bed under the sink. Somehow I've made it through the day. I tear at the bandages because my arms are on fire. I try to pull my plait out of my uniform pocket to hold in case I'm dying, only I'm not wearing my uniform and my hands are stiff, puppety paws. Maybe Malliane will hear me anyway.

And she does.

Because songs begin to straggle through my head. *Die proudly for Milea. The last of her line to boldly face the foe.* Each verse and refrain spins out effortlessly, like my namekin is singing right in my ear, and they're full of valor and courage and glittering eyes and lifted chins and other things that dying isn't. Dying is sweating and lying in a puddle of your own sick. It's not being able to stop shaking. It's your hair being all matted with tears because you want your ma and da and they're not coming. Not now. Not ever.

Emmy trades jobs with me so my bandages will stay somewhat dry and the burns can heal. Now I'm a bucket girl. I was sure Zoh would point wordlessly at my sink and hover her pencil over that clipboard, but she likely doesn't want the nuns asking too many questions about the bandages on my arms if they come down for an inspection. Not many things can get a prefect demerits, but a safety violation is one of them.

Bucket girls are in charge of replacing buckets of cold water at the washers' feet and removing full buckets at the wringers'. It's the most mindless job in the laundry and one of the most painful, given how much bending and stooping there is. There are worse things than being a bucket girl, though. Instead of being tied to a sink, I get to move around the room. I can chat with Gaddy and Emmy when Zoh's not looking, and I fool Cara by slinging empty buckets at her when she thinks they're full. I also don't have to put my hands back in water. Simply being near a sink makes my chewed-up forearms itch, and even though I know it's all in my head, I scratch them constantly.

It's a while before I take off the bandages. They're frayed like old ribbons and slimy from the aloe, but I've been stalling ever since Gaddy told me about a girl who got bluing burns on her hands that ate the flesh down to where they had to be amputated. The scarring starts just below my elbows, faint, in a scatter of pale grayish pits. By the time I unwrap as far as my forearms, my skin is red and hairless and cratered, and my hands themselves are claws, bony and papery.

I flex my fingers. They sting a little, but it's not nearly the relentless agony from that first day. They're stiff, but they bend and stretch and grab. They're still hands.

Malliane hasn't stopped watching over me. I haven't disappointed my name-kin completely.

Being a bucket girl turns your feet to wrinkly pulp and your back always aches, but you get to go outside, into the walled yard with the four pumps shared by the laundry, the kitchens, housekeeping, and janitorial. I'm in and out of the big heavy door a hundred times a day, pushing my rickety two-wheeled cart loaded down with buckets. The first time I opened the door, the tang of fresh air and the tickle of breeze and mud underfoot stopped me where I stood, and all I could do was breathe deep and shake my head at how sometimes costly things had unexpected silver linings.

There's a never-ending line for the pumps. Even though there are no nuns or novices below and prefects hardly ever leave their surveillance stations, no one talks. We're used to someone always listening, but down here there's just not that much to say. This is what it'll be like once we've *graduated*, whether we end up in a factory lodginghouse or servants' quarters. Chapped hands and dull silence and a weary sense that it could always be worse.

One day Fee appears, lugging a two-handled tub piled with bleachy rags. She wrings out cloth after cloth while another girl heaves the pump handle. They must be from janitorial. They're both pale, like they eat nothing but bread sandwiches and work longer hours than the kitchens and the laundry put together. When I think how clean the wash stations always were, how tidy the classrooms and perfect the dining hall, maybe that's not far from the truth.

Janitorial is ending her, and I'm the reason she's below. If I'd have just let the primer go, Jey would be the one standing here right now.

Or she might have kept quiet about it. Jey would have likely spent class carefully keeping any expression off her face and turning pages while wishing the same thing as me—to meet the girl who made this primer and find out how to become her. To resist, even in quiet ways, and stay Milean.

"Hey," I whisper to Fee. "You ever think of having a hedge school?"

Fee claws hair out of her face and mutters, "You've gotten me into enough trouble. Just stay away."

"You really need to listen to me," I reply. "This could change ev—"

Fee kneels to collect the rinsed-out rags, slaps them in the tub, then limps toward the door she came out of, her tub swaying from one raggedy, pale hand. I give up my place in line to tag after her, but she ignores me all the way across the yard and then shuts the door in my face. This girl was kind to me on my first day. She didn't inform on me when she had the chance. All I'm trying to do is help, and she won't even look me in the eye.

The next day I spot Fee in the pump line ahead of me, and the day after that she's behind me, but when I try to talk to her, even to say hello and ask how she's doing, she blanks her gaze like you do when a Wealdan is shouting at you for something. After a while, I leave her be. Maybe seeing me reminds her how she humiliated herself on the day we were sent below. Maybe she wants that moment back so she can stand songworthy beside me. If that's true, the best thing I can do is stay out of her conscience.

After a while, I'm strong enough to wheel a cart topped

up with six full buckets. Nothing hurts when I roll off my pallet under the sorting tables in the morning, and I barely even need to sleep anymore. The soles of my feet have hardened into hooves from the constant exposure to water, and I've stopped caring that I haven't seen the inside of a wash station in who even knows how many days.

After a while, class and the Cur estate and the chambers and the scarves feel like a song I heard once and then forgot the words to. Which is just as well. It's not like I'm going to see any of that for a long time—and if Fee can be believed, maybe never again.

One day I'm kneeling by the cart wheel in the pump yard, trying to replace the axle pin, when Fee crouches beside me. "I didn't think you were cruel. A loudmouth, yes. A troublemaker? Maybe, but enough time at Forswelt and you'd have figured things out like the rest of us. But mean enough to suggest I *just go to hedge school* when I can barely stand up at the end of the day? That's not like you. Or at least so I thought."

I fumble the pin into the mud. "What? No! I'd never—no, Fee, I meant it. You could start a hedge school." I hesitate, then add, "We did. In the laundry."

She rolls her eyes and struggles to stand, her knees making a nasty popping sound, but I grab her sleeve and nudge her toward the end of the pump line, away from the others. Fee studies the sky over the high wall, shaking her head bitterly. "No. I should have seen it. I should have said something. You were obsessed with Jasperine's primer. I thought it would help you. I never thought you'd take things this far."

I lick my lips, then croak, "Wh-what?"

"Well, more properly her great-granddaughter's. Tareliane. But everyone calls it Jasperine's primer." Fee sighs impatiently. "You can't think you're the only girl at Forswelt to find that book, can you?"

"But Loe made the primer. Didn't she?"

"Loe?" Fee coughs a laugh. "She wishes!"

I flap my lips for long moments. I was so sure, and Loe never corrected me there in the hallway of the Cur estate with a dusting rag in her hand. Finally I manage, "If Tareliane got sent below like us, she must still be here. Is she in janitorial with you? I want to meet her. I want—"

"You know how we all have numbers? Tareliane's number was 1. The very first girl to be enrolled at Forswelt National School, at swordpoint by graycoats. She lasted a week before getting sent to the workhouse."

Of course she did. The only way you make it out of national school a Milean is in a detention wagon.

"How do you know Tareliane made the primer, though?" I ask, but maybe Fee was here already. Maybe she came when the schools first opened and the Crown offered a season's rent forgiveness to parents who willingly complied with the Education Act, to celebrate the first of the emperor's reforms and his second year on the throne.

"No one remembers it not being here," Fee says, "so it must have been made by a girl in that first class. Who else but the great-granddaughter of Jasperine Vesley would have done such a thing?"

Other girls have joined the pump line behind us, and even though they look wrung out and dead on their feet, I lower my voice. "If Tareliane got sent to the workhouse over the primer, why was it still around for me to find? Wouldn't the nuns have destroyed it?"

"It wasn't the primer," Fee replies. "She got sent because she just . . . wouldn't. She refused to do anything. Go to class or vocational training, eat sandwiches, leave her hair unbound. Even use the wash station."

"What about her chambermates?"

"Those girls did the same thing. They made a pact. They'd be ungovernable—that's how the word got here from morality court, you know. One of them had it from her schoolmaster."

I pull in a tiny choke of breath. I had *ungovernable* from mine, too. Unless it was the same man. Unless Master Grenallan had the great-grandbabies of the Roll of Honor in his hedge schools and taught them no different than the rest of us.

"The four of them went together to the workhouse," Fee says. "They weren't going to play along with the demerits and the ranks and the scarves. At the end they were sitting in their chamber, refusing to . . . you know, visit the privy. It took six nuns and Captain Lennart of the constabulary to pull them out."

My jaw drops. "But that's what I tried to do! What I tried to get us all to do!"

"What you tried to *make* us do," Fee replies, and it's not bitter as much as it is sad.

"It was the songworthy thing," I insist. "We were all going down anyway!"

"Maybe," Fee says, "but you had this idea in your head about how we should go down—how *you* wanted to go down—so you did it without a thought for the rest of us."

I open my mouth to tell her she's wrong, but I'm the reason she's below in the first place, and it's not because she didn't do the songworthy thing. It's not because she didn't do what I said. She was resisting in her own way—not informing, not lording her first-rank scarf over me, not turning her back when I couldn't stop crying. I had no right to decide for her how she should resist.

No one followed Everard because he told them to. No one followed Jasperine at all. Even my da said nothing when people ate food that made them sick instead of stealing and risking the whip and morality court. He let them go their own way.

Maybe Gaddy was right. There's resistance all around me, and just because it's not how I'm doing it doesn't mean it's not resistance. Someone else had it figured out, and she left me a seditious primer so I'd know I wasn't alone. A tiny bound braid in my uniform pocket brought my name-kin back to me, even here at national school where I was supposed to be forgetting her every time I ran a brush through my ripply unbound hair. Only Malliane wouldn't know me anymore. Not now.

No Milean would.

Later, after the gaslight has been cut and before it's time for hedge school, I shake out my filthy tangle of hair. I tug loose a series of sections on the underside at the base of my neck, each as wide as a finger, and I plait them smooth and sure into Malliane's pattern. It'll be well hidden under the rest of my hair. A braid in my pocket isn't enough. It's got to be the hair on my head or I don't have name-kin. I won't be Milean, and if I'm not Milean, I might as well not be alive, and I very much want to be alive.

As I plait, I weave in a promise: Every girl at Forswelt can go her own way, and whatever happens, I will never again insist that someone else follow a path I've chosen for myself.

One morning I'm rolling a cartload of full buckets inside and reciting my lesson in my head—it'll be my turn to present at hedge school tonight—when Zoh waves me over to the surveillance station, where Sister Gunnhild and Novice Lilac are waiting.

I stop short. An inspection. I've done nothing wrong

and everything wrong. I swallow hard and look them both in the feet.

"1076, you've fulfilled the conditions of your correctional assignment," Sister Gunnhild says. "We're satisfied with reports of your progress, and in light of recent events, we've decided you're ready to rejoin your fellow students. Your demerit total will be set to twenty and you'll be given a fourth-rank bed, effective immediately."

A bed. A real bed and not a musty pallet under a sorting table. There'll be food, too, even if it's sandwiches, enough food that I can eat till I'm full. I can sit on my backside in a classroom and turn the pages of a book instead of hauling buckets everywhere like a workhouse inmate, and I'll never have to be near bluing again.

In light of recent events.

That makes no sense. I've done nothing special or noteworthy. If anything, I deserve demerits by the ton for not only attending an illegal school, but encouraging others to start one—to say nothing of binding my hair. Worse, Zoh is looking cheeky and smug, holding her clipboard protectively against her chest like she knows I can read a whole lot better after so many hedge school sessions stumbling through reports she carelessly dropped in the trash.

"Is this because of what happened with the bluing, honora?" I hold out my pitted, half-healed arms and snake a hard glance at Zoh. "The *safety violation*?"

Sister Gunnhild frowns. "667 has told us how you

misused a dangerous chemical despite her careful instructions, and how she had to demote you to bucket girl for your own safety. So no, your incident is irrelevant to our decision. I hope you learned a lesson, though."

Zoh is smirking. I can barely see straight. I've never wanted so badly to smack anyone in the mouth.

"There's an open fourth-rank bed in chamber 10, honora," Novice Lilac is saying to Sister Gunnhild. "Shall I take 1076 there?"

It'll be today. Right now. I can't even say good-bye.

"Take her to the wash station first." Sister Gunnhild wrinkles her nose. "Issue her new undergarments as well. That shift she's wearing should go straight to the incinerator."

My friends are scrubbing and wringing as if nothing unusual is happening, but Gaddy's eyes are red and Emmy has turned so her hair covers her face. These girls have been down here for months. Some of them for years. Here I am, getting out after only a short while, and for no reason anyone can tell, least of all me. It's unfair, and another time I'd have planted both feet and refused to go without them, or at least without an explanation, but I've learned my lesson. I make decisions for myself, not for other people.

Novice Lilac sighs impatiently, so instead of rushing around hugging my friends, which would likely get us all in trouble, I pull my uniform out from under the counter and follow her up ramps and down hallways and finally into the wash station. She has a clean uniform over her arm, and while I fumble through the pocket of my old one and gather my bound plait into my fist, she inks my number beneath the Embattled Crown on the front of the new one. My heart is racing with every stroke of her pen, because all she has to do is tell me to open my hand and I am lost. But she doesn't, and when she's gone, I slip my bound plait into the new uniform pocket, all the way to the bottom.

Then I stand for what feels like hours under a hot shower. It's odd to be here alone, but nice, too, and I scrub off a second skin of sweat-caked dirt and grime. Whole chunks of grit slither down the drain when I wash my hair. As I rinse, my fingers catch on the plait. The one buried in the underside of my hair. The one that'll get me shorn along with my three new chambermates if I'm caught.

Only I can't make myself unplait it. I run my fingers down it, wet and sleek and bumpy in the pattern I've known how to weave since I was barely out of diapers. Now that it's in, unplaiting it feels like blasphemy. Like I'm forgetting my name-kin and turning my back on my Milean family, just like the Education Act says I should for the sake of my future in the Wealdan empire.

I rub soap into the plait, then shake the rest of my wet hair over it.

My old trunk is waiting in chamber 10 when I arrive damp and clean and smelling delightfully of lanolin. Someone from housekeeping brought it invisibly and thanklessly. I've probably nodded at her below in the pump yard. An orange fourth-rank scarf is piled on top, and I settle it around my neck. There's a bundle of linens on the empty bed, and my hands crimp up in sympathy when I think of the number of girls who touched those bedclothes from the time they left someone's chamber, slept in, to the time they arrived here, clean. I definitely know those girls. I might have been one of them.

"Make your bed," Novice Lilac says. "Then you'll need to report to Sister Chlotilde's classroom. Can you find it on your own?"

I nod. I learned Wealdan numerals from those same reports Zoh threw away.

"Here. Your hall pass." Novice Lilac writes on her demerit pad, hands me the paper, and turns to leave.

It's probably a bad idea, but I can't stop myself from asking, "Honorata? Why was I excused from correction?"

"The same reason as anyone else," Novice Lilac says in a curious level tone, and disappears without another word.

Bewildered, I make my bed and head to the instruction wing. A burly redheaded girl answers my knock and swings the classroom door. Three steps in, I freeze. The tables have been pushed against the walls, and two girls I don't know are alone at the front of the room, saying something about morality court in stilted, uncomfortable voices. The others are sitting on the floor like they're in chapel listening to a sermon.

Sister Chlotilde stands up in the back of the room where her desk has been moved. I brace for rage, but she grins like a cat on the hunt. "Oh, good. My new Hock Cur is here."

"Wh-what?" I go cold all over.

Sister Chlotilde smiles. "You've been reassigned. The girl who was originally chosen to play General Hock Cur . . . let's just say she's no longer my problem. So that honor falls to you. General Cur happens to be a personal hero of mine, so you'd better do an extra-good job portraying him. . . ."

The nun keeps talking, but there's a roaring in my ears and a sick taste in the back of my mouth. Cav Horn would have been buried under six feet of Milean earth without Hock Cur. Cav Horn was merely a competent soldier out for adventure and loot. Hock Cur was the man who wasn't going home without a coronet and an estate to rival the empress's.

Somehow I'm still on my feet. "Honora. I'm a stagehand. I can't—"

"Shut up. You've been given your role. You're going to play it."

"But . . ." I choke. "My audition was terrible. I messed up all those lines."

Sister Chlotilde's grin goes cold. "Believe me, 1076, you weren't chosen because of the quality of your audition."

If a girl ever amasses enough demerits to earn a second correctional vocational sentence, she will be sent to the workhouse, as it will be clear that the first one taught her nothing.

My knees give out. My backside hits the floor hard enough to jolt my whole body. Now I see what those recent events were that got me out of the laundry. The girl who was playing Hock Cur resisted openly and was disappeared, and now I've got the part for only one reason—I can't afford to make trouble.

"So." Sister Chlotilde rocks away from the desk and aims her crop at the class. "You'll notice 401 isn't here anymore. In case any of you thought I was kidding when I warned you about your attitudes."

A fourth-rank bed opened up in chamber 10. Because the girl who woke up in it this morning is on her way to the workhouse right now.

Nim sits quietly by herself in the corner. She looks like she hasn't slept in weeks, and her bright Wealdan hair looks even shinier, like the nuns gave her special soap for it. When Sister Chlotilde says "attitudes," she flinches like someone slapped her.

"It wasn't easy convincing Sister Gunnhild that I should direct this play," Sister Chlotilde says into the silence, "but no one in this whole place knows more about history than I do. *Definitely* no one cares about it more. So you dimwits need to understand something. This production of *The Winning of New Weald* will be a moving and glorious and fitting tribute to the majesty of the Crown and the greatness of the empire. There's no other option. Am I making myself perfectly clear?"

The class mumbles, "Yes, honora," and somehow my mouth does too.

"Good. 1076 is playing General Cur now. She has a lot of catching up to do. You people are supposedly so great at memorizing things. Let's see how well she remembers the script from before. 13, 1076, take the stage."

Nim stands up slowly, leaning on the wall like her legs are jelly. I join her at the front of the room, but the shock of the day settles on me and a sourness crawls up the back of my throat. I do remember Hock Cur's lines. Every skin-crawling one of them. I also remember that his costume will be an army coat covered in pigtails made of braided string to make it *historically accurate,* because taking trophies wasn't illegal till the Relief Act.

"The first scene," Sister Chlotilde says, "where Cav Horn and Hock Cur make landfall. Let's see it. Now."

It feels like another life ago when I gave my terrible audition. When I tried to convince everyone else to do it too. I was so sure it would work, that if we only did the songworthy thing, everything would turn out like a song. Now that I've lived a song or two, nothing is as simple as they'd have us believe. The plan I had all those days and weeks ago would never have worked anyway, and for the first time, I'm glad no one else went through with it. I'd have taken a whole lot more people below with me.

This play isn't going to happen. I'm not going to say the lines they've given me. This time I'll sabotage the play myself, and I'll make it look like an accident so no one gets in trouble.

Especially me. Forswelt doesn't need a martyr. Once you're a martyr, that's all you are. What this school needs is someone who'll resist. Someone who's not afraid to fight alone and doesn't need to take credit for doing the right thing.

Someone ungovernable.

At lunch I meet my new chambermates. First-rank Pev is bluff and cheerful, the kind of girl who talks too loud and smiles a lot and wants everyone to be happy and get along. Third-rank Mor has a fluffy cloud of black hair, and even though she's little, she eats more food than all of us put together. Our second is Jey, and I can tell they're still working on the stage because she's a deep bronze from the sun, and I'm so jealous I can barely see straight. Jey makes a squinchy face and opens her hands like an offering, then says, *I can't tell you how sorry I am. I had no idea.*

All I had to do was let her have that primer. All I had to do was trust her. I didn't, so I sign with my scarred hands, *I shouldn't have done what I did. I want to apologize, too. No hard feelings. Really.* And I mean it.

I'm also sorry you got dragged out of correction to play the Butcher of the Burning Days, she adds, looking like she just ate something sour.

I shrug, but it's hard to force down the mouthful of sandwich I'm chewing.

"Never thought I'd be glad to be stuck in costuming." Pev signs for Jey as she speaks, so they've clearly been chambermates awhile. "Although today I had to gather the shirts and tunics that the Milean *peasants* will be wearing and trample them through the mud. I had to do it three times before Sister Radegund said they were *historically accurate*." She rolls her eyes so Jey will get her meaning.

"I have to paint sets." Mor signs as she talks as well. "Pictures of things like the chapel at Victory Hill and the insides of factories. I kind of want to ruin them." Then she scowls and adds in a low voice, "No, I *really* want to ruin them."

I sit up straighter. Pev mutters dark things into her salad, and Jey is violently stabbing her tofu with a butter knife. This is a world away from the reluctant compliance I remember from before I was sent below. So I venture, signing as I go, "Aren't you *excited* for this production? It's an honor, after all, because the viceroy could be anywhere on Expansion Day."

Jey scowls. *No. It's rubbish. That's what it is.*

After lunch, we separate and head to our different production areas. My chambermates have no reason to lie, but it's still hard to believe I heard right. None of them bothered to hide how they felt about the play. It would be so much easier to sabotage it with help.

Only this is starting to sound familiar, and I won't tell other people what to do and expect them to do it, even if it's the songworthy thing. I'm definitely not going to put people in danger again. I get to decide things for me and no one else.

Still, now that I know to look, I notice eye rolls and foot dragging during afternoon rehearsal. Girls are deliberately not hitting their marks, which is stage talk for knowing when to stand where, and they mess up the blocking and bump into other actors. It's enough to get them a yelling-at by Sister Chlotilde and the occasional cropping, but not enough for demerits.

It's definitely resistance.

Nim and I are supposed to be working on the first scene, the one where we're together on the *Inevitable* talking about how these green fields will enrich our great empire. If I was being historically accurate, I'd be saying how we're here to steal enough land so we can stand in front of the empress as her peers instead of her subjects. Only, Nim can't stop trembling. She's so pale I can all but see through her.

". . . this banner in the sand," I recite, "and claim this land as New Weald." I wait, but Nim only cinches her arms over her chest and closes her eyes. "Nim? Your line."

She shakes her head. Shivers like it's winter. Sister Chlotilde is across the room, brimming with rage at three girls playing inquisitors. I angle my body so the nun can't see Nim and say, "You all right? You look sick. Maybe you should go to the infirmary."

"No way. Not going there."

"All right. Fair enough." I wish I could hug her, just once, even quickly, because being alone here is really hard. "Look. This whole thing? This stupid production? Don't worry, all right?"

Nim snorts and echoes mockingly, *"Don't worry.* Do I look *worried?"*

"You look like you're dying," I reply, and I say it teasing, but Nim flinches hard and digs her fingernails into her arms.

"Maybe I am. Maybe being Cav Horn is killing me."

Even though I haven't exactly decided what I'm going to do yet, I know I'm doing something, and I'd be a wreck too if I thought I'd have to stand in front of everyone as Hock Cur. Nim's had to do it for *weeks.* I lean close and mutter, "When I say don't worry, I mean the viceroy might be coming to Forswelt, but he'll be disappointed if he thinks he'll be watching a production."

Nim peers at me sidelong. "Do not joke about that."

I shake my head solemnly, and Nim's eyes go wide.

"So do what you can to give your lines. The nuns can't know anything's going on. And trust me when I tell you not to worry."

"Trust you?" Nim lifts her chin, looking something other than wrecked for the first time today. "If you're really putting a stop to this, I'll be helping you."

"But I—"

"Because I am *not* doing this," Nim hisses. "Everyone here thinks they know all about me. It does no good to tell people my parents are Milean, my grands were Milean, and I'm unlucky enough to have a single Wealdan ancestor who came over with Cav freaking Horn and decided to make himself a part of my family and stick me with this stupid, stupid hair." She bares her teeth into a dangerous smile. "So if I have to get up in front of everyone and say this butcher's lines, that's all anyone will remember when they see me for the rest of my time here. When I'm sleeping in the bed next to them. Standing in the wash station with my back to them and water in my eyes."

I did think that. I didn't for a moment try to put myself where she is, a Milean girl who has the bad luck to look Wealdan, trying to make her way in a place where we're encouraged to turn our backs on one another—or turn on one another outright.

"So if you're going to ruin this production, I will help you." Nim grips her script hard enough to crumple. "I'll take demerits over it. I'll go to the workhouse over it."

"I can't ask you to do that," I murmur.

"You didn't. You don't have to."

I start to tell her that she can't. That what I'm doing is for me alone, and no one else should risk herself. But if I don't get to tell girls what they have to do, I sure as anything don't get to tell them what they *can't* do. If Nim is allowed go her own way, and the way she wants to go is the same one as mine, all I can do is be glad for the company, even if I think she's making a huge mistake.

We spend the rest of rehearsal quietly discussing how we'll sabotage the production, and hopefully, the viceroy's entire visit. For all her bold talk, Nim quickly agrees that whatever we do should look like an accident and end up with no one getting hurt or caught. We just don't agree what that would look like.

When rehearsal is over and Sister Chlotilde starts collecting scripts, Nim whispers, "We'll have to meet later. I'm in chamber 39. After second bed check, tap on the door three times. It's at the end of the corridor, so we'll be able to talk in the alcove."

"Why can't you come to my chamber?"

"Because if you get caught out after bed check, you'll get demerits and your chambermates will be annoyed. If I rack any up, my chambermates will try to kill me." She tugs the neckline of her uniform down to show an ugly raised scar over her collarbone. "The one across my stomach is worse and newer, but I can't show you without flashing everyone."

I crack a reluctant smile, but it's mostly because I don't know what to say. Resisting costs her more. We don't all come to this equally.

A bed-check violation can't be worth more than a demerit. Two at the most, random or not, and Sister Gunnhild said my total would be set at twenty when I left correction. The nuns might be holding the workhouse over my head to make sure I behave, but we're getting close enough to Expansion Day that they can't keep dragging girls out of correction and expecting them to play a flawless Hock Cur. They want the production to be a success a lot more than they want to send anyone else to the workhouse, and I'm doing a decent job of convincing them I'm complying. Besides, after seeing that scar, I can hardly tell Nim that I can't risk demerits either, so I reply, "All right. Be ready."

After lights-out, I sing outlawed songs in my head to keep myself awake, but I must have shut my eyes for a moment because the next thing I know, the door is being pulled closed from outside and the wedge of faint gaslight from the hallway is narrowing. I mutter a swear. I missed seeing which novice counted us, so I don't know if that was first or second bed check. I put on my robe and pad to the end of the hall, listen for novices, then hurry upstairs and tap on the door of chamber 39.

Nothing.

I wait, shifting from foot to foot, but I don't want to knock again in case I wake Nim's chambermates. She's going to think I got scared. Maybe even that I informed on her. So I wait some more. Nim's got it hard enough here without me turning on her too.

Or maybe she changed her mind. Maybe she heard me and isn't going to answer the door.

It's a long while before I make myself head back to my chamber. I'm cold and tired and there's a hard lump in my belly because I really thought something would come of this. I must have waited too long, because I'm coming around the corner into the corridor when a shadow slips out of the dark and darts over to chamber 10.

Nim. It has to be. This isn't the plan. She should have stuck to the plan. My chambermates are going to be upset. Because it's Nim, they might even do something awful. I fly up the corridor on soundless bare feet just in time for the shadow to tap on the door in an odd pattern and whisper, "We are ungovernable girls" to whoever slides it open a thumbswidth. I shove in behind her. Already a story is coming together in my head. Nim and I arranged to rehearse our scenes late. I'm weeks behind everyone and Sister Chlotilde is terrifying and we didn't want to put anyone in danger.

But the girl who came in isn't Nim. Her hair's nowhere near as curly. She moves away from the door to another set of girl-shaped shadows near my bed.

"Sorry about this." Nim pushes the door shut and the room goes dim again. "I had no way to let you know the plan needed changing, so I had to risk coming here. It should tell you something that they came anyway even though I'm the one who told them."

A chill runs through me. *Them.* I spark the gaslight and turn it on the lowest setting—and suck in a breath. There are nearly twenty girls in our chamber. Crowded on our beds, shoulder to shoulder, lining the walls in the tiny amount of walking space in the room, wide-eyed and fidgeting and trembling, all of them risking dozens of demerits for at least three different infractions, conspiracy being the worst of them.

"What are you all doing here?" I breathe.

"The costumes are already two weeks behind schedule," Pev says quietly. "The patterns went missing. Then we broke every pair of scissors. I thought we were the only ones, though."

Mor shakes her head. "You're not. Someone left all the paintbrushes overnight in turpentine a while back and the bristles fell out. The nuns were furious, but we played dumb and they just huffed and had us put together new ones. We made an afternoon's work take a whole week because we're stupid Mileans who don't know how to use glue."

"You . . . you're not complying?" I ask slowly. I spot Jey looking peeved, so I risk turning up the gaslight another notch and start signing. "You're sabotaging the play on your own?"

There's a ripple of motion through the room as girls nod, some grimly and some nervously and some with just the hint of a smirk.

It's one thing for Nim to risk herself. Another thing entirely for this roomful of girls to be one informer away from a trip below, or worse. I turn to her and ask, "What did you tell them?"

"That you were bringing the whole production to a standstill," Nim replies, "and you have been ever since your terrible audition."

I fall against the wall for support. I don't have a plan. Not even a half-baked one, and my ridiculous audition did more harm than good. Yet on the potential alone, almost two dozen girls showed up after bed check and crowded into my chamber, just like those farmers from the Burning Days who lost their land to freebooters, who found Everard already fighting against the Wealdan advance and offered to join him.

Jey leans past me to turn up the gaslight again. *Kem, we need this. Please don't say Brassyhead here got it wrong. It was hard enough driving nails when I thought the production would happen.* She makes a sad little open-handed shrug. *Let us help.*

"Let you?" It's coming back now, the habit of signing as I speak. "I'm not in charge. No one has to do anything. But if you're going the same way as me, we can all go together. Also? I'm done with imperial names. I'm Malley. At least when there are no nuns or novices around."

The room goes tremble-quiet. Because I spoke those words in Milean. And it's likely that the last time any of these girls heard Milean was their parents sobbing as they were loaded onto school wagons all those months or years ago. Not everyone gets pulled into a makeshift hedge school run by exhausted but ungovernable girls long after lights-out. Not everyone knows it's possible to resist in such a way, to keep days and days from ending them like they could have ended me in the laundry.

Then Jey says, *You sure you're not in charge? Every flying column needs a commander.*

I snort, because she's clearly being funny. "I don't remember being elected commander. What, you hoping to make field captain?"

Jey doesn't giggle or smirk. Instead she gestures at the girls packed into our chamber, taking the biggest risk of their lives, and asks, *You think Everard wanted to be in charge?*

Maybe he didn't. Maybe Everard stood where I am now, faced with dozens of people pushed beyond a point where they could bring themselves to comply. Those farmers didn't come to him because they thought he could get their land back. They came because they couldn't live knowing they'd done nothing to resist, and Everard gave them hope that something could come of it, even if that something was songworthy acts for the ungovernable to remember.

He could have turned them away. Everard Talshine could have told them the rumors were wrong, that there was no one in the mountains wrecking everything Wealdan he could get to. Just like I can tell these girls they should keep their heads down and avoid demerits instead of standing up for themselves because it finally hurts enough.

He didn't, though. Instead he formed those men and women into a sleek, orderly resistance force. It was the first of many, but without question the most effective. Everard's Flying Column came into being when one ordinary farmer realized that if people were going the same way he was, they'd all be better off if someone held them together.

DAY 145

AT BREAKFAST SISTER GUNNHILD READS OUT the day's schedule. I've been in rehearsals for five days in a row, so I'll be heading to instruction in the morning and vocational training in the afternoon. Getting the production together has made everything topsy-turvy—it took me a while to work out how long I'd been below—and girls from all four ranks are thrown together at random without their chambermates so the nuns can still comply with the Education Act, which mandates how much instruction we get while also making sure the Curs don't have to wash their own dishes or scrub their own privies.

I report to classroom 8 as directed, where a nun I've never met smiles bright and pleasant as she asks what reading group I'm in. I'm not used to nuns being kind, so it's a moment before I manage, "Beginning, honora."

"Splendid!" She says it like a I'm a pet or a toddler, and she clearly doesn't notice how I'm gripping my skirt to still my hands because even though Master Grenallan taught us how to lie with a straight face, I never could get rid of all my tells. "Why don't you get a primer and find a seat?"

A primer. I blink away sudden tears, because I should have said intermediate. That way I'd get a stupid storybook with no pictures to remind me how awful and selfish I was. I choose a primer at random and take it to my table. Just holding it feels like the same failure as that first day, when I unbound all my pigtails and stood nameless and helpless and compliant. Jasperine's great-granddaughter must have felt that way too, but she didn't slink to her seat and do as she was told.

Only schoolmasters can make new songs, but I can remake this primer. In honor of the ungovernable girls at Forswelt who came before me, who gave me hope, and for all the girls who'll come after me, even if I'm not here to meet them. They'll need to know they can resist, and not just in costly ways. They'll need to know they're not alone.

Me, I'm going to need a stick of drawing lead. The permanent kind.

So that afternoon I steal one from Maude Cur's huge, ridiculous desk. It's not even difficult. When the surveillance nun is at the opposite end of the corridor, I walk into the captain's office with my half-full bucket of wash water like I have every reason to be there. The room is empty, and blocks of glorious sunlight glide through the floor-to-ceiling windows and spread over the plush blue rug. There's an enamel cup on the edge of the desk that's full of writing things, and I grab a lead stick and weave it into the plait hidden in the underside of my hair. Then I'm out the door, bucket in hand, heading toward the next privy down, trying not to grin. We're never searched, either coming or going to vocational training, but I can only breathe again once I've safely stashed the drawing lead at the bottom of my trunk.

That night, in the wash station, I put my mouth under the faucet and drink as much water as I can. It's well past second bed check when I blink awake and have to pee. I put on my robe, pocket my drawing lead, and cautiously push the chamber door open. The hallway is empty, dimly gaslit at the end where there's a privy stall. I use it, which is allowed, then check the area for novices before padding down the hall toward the classrooms. Which definitely isn't.

I go right to classroom 8 and grab a primer. The window lets in a pale shaft of moonlight that's just enough to see by. I pull out the drawing lead and turn to *O is for Ocean*.

I studied the pictures in the seditious primer down to the tiniest detail, but re-creating them is harder than I thought. My nuns look like potatoes in habits, and my gray-coats are tubby squares with round heads and sticky-out ears. They don't look like they're drowning in the ocean at all, just lying on top of it. I grit my teeth and rub out their faces with the end of my robe, then make their mouths bigger and x out their eyes. A little better, but Tareliane made them look terrified and defeated, struggling against the ropes and rocks that dragged them mercilessly down. She made them look like no one was coming to help them. Not now. Not ever.

My pictures don't have to be as good as hers. They simply have to be there, waiting for the next girl who needs them. This time, I won't hold on to my seditious primer so hard. This time I will open my hand and share it, just as Jasperine's great-granddaughter intended.

DAY 149

DURING REHEARSAL, WHILE SISTER CHLOTILDE
yells at the girl playing Johan Rule about her attitude, I
plan my new picture. *N is for National School,* burning to
the ground with all the nuns and novices panicking inside.
After second bed check, I'm heading down the darkened
corridor when out of nowhere I stumble over something
soft and piled-up, like someone dropped her cloak in the
middle of the hallway. I muffle a squeal and brace to hit the
ground loud and hard, but someone grabs my arms. Novices. Novices who must have been watching me and know—

"Hold it!" A girl whose voice I recognize, her whisper
fierce and savage. "Just hear us out, Kem. Please."

Loe. That's Loe's voice, and Koa is the one breathing in

my ear. Ordinarily I'd be interested in anything you have to talk about after lights-out and away from the someones who are always listening, but my mind is entirely on my primer. I let them shuffle me through a cracked-open classroom door and out of any passing novice's line of sight, but when I don't let them push me farther in than that, they let me loose. Both seem impatient, glancing at the door every other moment, but not angry like they want a fight or smug like they're about to inform.

It's dawning on me that the cloak I tripped on wasn't dropped at random. They've been watching me sneak around, so they knew where I'd be and they set a trap.

Loe must see me reach for the doorknob, because she leans close and says, "Kem, we need you with us. The honor girls. We need you."

The honor girls. Loe and Koa and the rest of that shadowy outfit, each of them with a grand or an ancestor on the Roll of Honor. Who absolutely *do not* meet in secret, and even if they did, it wouldn't be for me.

"What's this about?" I ask cautiously.

"You've seen that big stupid throne being built near the stage?" Loe grins. "We're bringing it down. With the viceroy in it."

"But—he could get hurt."

Koa snorts. "You of all people shouldn't give one hairy fig about the viceroy getting hurt."

"I care about the stagehands getting blamed for it," I

reply sharply. "I care about my friends being sent to the workhouse."

Loe tucks a nail into my palm and gestures for me to break it. I frown, but I try anyway, and it snaps in two like a brittle twig.

"That viewing box the viceroy will sit in?" Koa says. "The one that's going up now? We need you to swap out the good nails for these bad ones without the stagehands knowing, and we need you to get us good nails so we can ruin them. When the throne collapses, it'll look like the nuns didn't provide the stagehands with decent building materials. And of course *we* wouldn't know any better."

"We can only make these weak nails in small batches," Loe adds. "So you have to convince the stagehands to slow things down even more. The fewer good nails they use, the better the chance that this will work."

For a long moment I picture it. That throne coming down with a splintery crash. The viceroy breaking his neck on the very ground his ancestors stole from us. Nuns and novices weeping and flailing and rushing around in a panic. And Koa's right—if the viceroy was to get hurt and none of us were blamed and the production canceled, that would be the best Expansion Day ever.

". . . called off immediately," Loe is saying. "Whatever you're planning. One bad thing happening at the production is an accident. Two? I think we all know where we'd end up."

Loe has a plan. An actual plan. One that's got a good

chance of working, unlike the haphazard slow-down, mess-up approach we've been taking for lack of something better. But the way she says it makes me ask, "How do you know I'm planning something?"

"It's all anyone talks about," Loe says. "In the wash stations. In the dining hall. I've even overheard my chambermates whispering about it after lights-out, and these are girls who once just wanted to go to class and training and earn their yearly visit with their parents. They don't want trouble. But they're listening to you."

I giggle helplessly. They might be listening to me, but I don't have much to say that's useful. "Why don't you just ask the girls doing set construction to use the bad nails and get you good ones to wreck? My chambermate is one of them. Jey. You can sign, right? She—"

"We tried that," Loe cuts in. "Jey wouldn't take the nails unless I told her why. She doesn't trust me. Me! My great-grandda was Everard Talshine and *she* doesn't trust *me*."

"Jey trusts *you*, though," Koa adds. "She would convince the other stagehands to do it if you were the one who asked her."

"Then she told me something about being a field captain, like you were running a flying column or something." Loe groans. "Honestly! If anyone's going to run a flying column around here, it ought to be the girl whose ancestor practically invented them."

I bristle at Loe's accusing look, because I'm trying to

agree with her and help her. "I'll talk to Jey. The other girls too. They should hear your plan, but I bet they'll love it. They'll be lining up to help you."

"We're not asking them. We're asking you."

My mouth falls open, but Loe rushes on, "Not that we have anything against them. But they're not . . ."

"What?" I lift my chin. "Honor girls? Neither am I. You said as much."

Koa sighs. "You can't tell the stagehands they're building with bad nails. The more people who know, the more likely it is the nuns will find out."

"You told Jey."

"The only thing I told her was to stop building with any nails but the ones I gave her," Loe says impatiently. "I really didn't think she'd be so difficult."

"Do all the honor girls know?" I ask.

"Well . . . yes." Loe sounds puzzled.

"So you just don't trust us ordinary girls not to talk." I narrow my eyes. "I do. You should too."

"You can tell them something's going to happen," Loe says. "You can give them that. They've had enough, same as the rest of us. It's not fair to take away their hope."

"They already know something's going to happen," I say, "because they're all working together to make it happen."

Loe grits her teeth. "We can't risk it. Call it off, whatever it is. They'll listen to you."

"They won't tell," I insist.

"They need us, and we need you with us."

"I'm not an honor girl," I reply sourly.

"You will be," Loe says in a quiet voice, "if you join us."

The classroom is kind of pleasant in the middle of the night. The tables are lined up nice and orderly, and that patch of moonlight is always on the floor like it's waiting for me. I pull my seditious primer off the shelf, but then I sit outside the moonlight with the cover still closed. My ma and da would burst their buttons with pride if I fell in with the great-granddaughter of Everard Talshine, but I can't turn my back on girls who are already risking so much to sabotage the production. Loe's wrong about one thing— they already know the production isn't going to happen. It shouldn't matter one bit if they know about the honor girls' plan to bring down the viceroy.

Which means Loe is trying to get me to do what she wants when it's not what I want, and she's offering a privilege for my compliance.

Songs start running through my head, jumbled up with the names of the ungovernable on the Roll of Honor, all of which are the only way I know my ancestors didn't just kneel and comply.

That's how you end up with nothing. When you can't bring the best parts of the past with you into the future.

Loe stood in the hallway of the Cur estate dusting a portrait of some ridiculous Wealdan nobleman and let me slobber all over her because her great-grandda was Everard Talshine, who led the very first flying column and turned back the Wealdan advance, and mine was a farmer named Grenval, who lasted twenty-two days in the workhouse.

We need a plan. Loe has a plan. It doesn't matter who came up with it. What matters is that the girls know their work sewing bad seams and dropping sawdust into paint isn't for nothing. They can keep showing up for rehearsal without breaking down or breaking noses because they know the production absolutely will not be happening. Once the viceroy eats dirt, the last thing he'll want will be to watch a bunch of sullen girls stomp around in ugly costumes. Assuming any of it is even ready.

We have a plan. Soon everyone will know it, and that will keep the production from ending us.

I pull the stick of drawing lead out of my pocket and settle down to start work on *A is for Abeya*. Only the furry orange creature already has a nun in its jaws, and there are nun corpses at its feet. Just like that first primer. Jasperine's primer.

I pull my lead away like the page burned me. Last night this picture was untouched. Someone else has been drawing in this primer.

That's impossible. Not just because no one else knows what I'm doing, but because this drawing is exactly like the one in the seditious primer I spent hours and hours studying like it was made just for me. This is Jasperine's primer. Someone saved it from the incinerator.

But that's impossible too. Sister Chlotilde would have burned it personally.

I flip to *O is for Ocean*. That drawing is mine. There are my awkward drowning nuns and graycoats who still look like they're floating with their x-ed-out eyes and wide, gaping mouths.

I turn back to *A is for Abeya* and squint hard at the picture in the silvery light. It's not the same as in the first primer. Not exactly. The nun hanging from the abeya's jaws is a little floppier and the blood pool is wider. Same with the baby. He still has Milean pigtails, but they're in a slightly different pattern and there are more of them.

My drawings are nowhere near as clever and lifelike as these, which are clearly new and definitely made by the same artist as the first primer, which was supposedly made by the great-granddaughter of Jasperine Vesley. Either Jasperine's great-granddaughter was never sent to the workhouse with her chambermates, or she didn't make this primer. Because whoever did is still here.

"She's been here all along," I say aloud into the empty classroom.

I hug my primer. I hug it tight. If she's still here, I can find her. Not because she's Jasperine's flesh and blood. Not because she can help me stay Milean at national school. Because we are going the same way, and she is clearly more songworthy than I will ever be.

DAY 150

WE START REHEARSING ON THE SET. SISTER Gerta rushes around, apologizing for its incompleteness, but it's finished enough for us to practice on. The stage itself is raised waist-high off the ground, about as big as a classroom, and at either end there's a wooden beam with a ring screwed in where a length of wire is strung to hang the backdrops. It looks so much like a gallows for hanging people that I shudder. There are are curtained-off areas on both ends of the stage where the actors will gather and wait for their turn to perform, but the audience won't be able to see.

The half-built throne for the viceroy dominates the whole area. It's got tall, skinny legs cluttered with a web of curlicues and filigree, and it's centered so it has a perfect view of the stage. There are lower viewing boxes on either side, likely where the war criminals will sit, and Jey is standing on the roof of one, barefoot and confident and gloriously sun-browned, driving nails into the throne with slow, reluctant *thwacks*.

I mutter a swear. The stagehands are further into the project than Loe let on. Somehow I'll have to convince them to undo all that work. More to the point, they'll have to figure out a reason to take the throne apart and start over that won't raise questions.

Hock Cur is in a lot of scenes, so I have to wait till the conclave of inquisitors meets to found the first morality court before I can drift over to the stagehands' water station and give Jey enough of a look that she'll join me.

We're not doing the production, right? she asks. *All this is for show. Right?*

Yes, I reply confidently, and I pull the bundle of bad nails far enough out of my pocket that she can see them. *If you and the stagehands start using only nails I give you.*

Jey frowns, openly suspicious, and says, *I told Loe there's no way I'm doing anything unless I have all the facts.*

So it's true, then. I scowl. *Loe asked you to use these nails to build the viceroy's throne and didn't say why.*

She didn't ask. She told. And she told me not to bother her with questions, either. That it was better if I didn't know. Like someone elected her commander of this flying column or something.

No one elected me, either, I reply, and I almost add how we're not a flying column, not really, not like Everard's, but maybe it's time to take something good out of the past and bring it into the present so we have a chance at a future. *Look, the honor girls did something to these nails, so if the stagehands use them to build the throne, it's going to collapse, hopefully with the viceroy in it. That's going to ruin the production outright. Yes, it's possible the stagehands will be blamed, but the Wealdans don't think we're capable of something like this. The Crown provided the blueprints, a clueless nun is supervising the build, and the supplies came from imperial warehouses.* I run a hand through my hair. *You absolutely don't have to do this, but I think it'll work.*

Behind me, on the stage, the conclave of inquisitors is all over the place, not even close to hitting their marks, and Sister Chlotilde is shoving and dragging girls into position. I shift from foot to foot, but Jey is still frowning and deciding. She needs time. It's the one thing I can give her.

It's a good plan, Jey finally says. *Loe should have just told me everything.* I'm nodding, agreeing completely, when Jey adds, *If I'd have known this was your idea all along, I wouldn't have given her such a hard time.*

Well, it— I stop, because Jey is taking the packet of nails out of my hand and peering thoughtfully at the half-built throne like she's figuring out how to go about compromising it. If we really are a flying column, it doesn't matter whose idea it is. I may not be commander, but Jey is definitely a field captain. Besides, Loe could be a lot less dismissive of my friends. She could trust them enough to keep secrets and not order them around. I tap Jey's shoulder for her attention and say, *The nails will come in batches. Stall the build as much as you can. The more of these nails in the throne, the better our chances.*

Jey drops the nails into her pocket. *That's going to be hard. Expansion Day is still two weeks away, and Sister Gerta has gone through a whole demerit pad.*

Do what you can, I reply, and Jey nods grimly and moves off toward her toolbox. I rejoin the actors in time to listen to three girls dressed in the nobility's robes of state talk about how glad they are that the winning of New Weald means that Wealdans are now free to turn their keen minds to philosophy, politics, art, and literature. Meanwhile, a handful of girls in filthy shirts and trousers pretend to dig with hoes.

"Smile!" Sister Chlotilde hisses at them. "You are happy to be given an honest day's work!"

After rehearsal, Sister Chlotilde stomps away to find Sister Gerta and complain about loose boards on the stage. We have to rake up wood shavings so the lawn is green and perfect. Before the production, this was when we often had free time, but since fourth rank was never allowed outside, chores are way better than sitting in a stifling room, counting my fingers and toes.

The afternoon is bright and smells like pine, and if I close my eyes it's like one of a million summer days in

Trelawney Crossing with my friends. My throat starts to hurt and I'm tired of crying over things like this, so I rake my small pile of wood chips into a bigger pile, then pose dramatically and say, "I am Hock Cur, Butcher of the Burning Days. I definitely wasn't stupid enough to almost get myself captured by Jasperine, who would have gleefully thrown me into the sea bound in chains and weighted with rocks like she did to some of my fellow graycoated brutes. That would not be historically accurate, because I'm the one who gets to decide what counts as history."

The other actors stop where they are. I didn't say it loudly and Sister Chlotilde is nowhere near, but I really should know by now what going my own way looks like.

But Ilo, one of the girls playing an inquisitor, grins and holds up her rake like a rifle. "I am Aurelia Cradlemore, but as far as historical accuracy is concerned, I never existed, because I actually held off Hock Cur's best murderers for six whole months until he rolled cannons up to my walled fort and leveled everything. I even winged him with a rifle I plundered off a graycoat, but that never happened because Hock Cur's *war injury* came about when he rescued one of his lieutenants from a rock slide. The empress herself pinned a medal on him for it too." Ilo aims her rake-rifle at me, still grinning. "Bang!"

I clap a hand against my shoulder and make a show of falling to my knees, whisper-wailing, "Help! History! Save me!"

The actors start laughing and making up their own new lines as they rake. Everard at that icy pass. The five sisters who became the Hanged Maidens after quietly poisoning the high-ranking graycoats who commandeered their homestead and demanded hospitality. I join them, still fighting down giggles and glancing around for nuns, but Nim has stopped working. She regards me long and level. "Let's do it."

"What do you mean?"

"The production," Nim replies in an odd, measured voice. "Let's do it your way. Make up our own lines. Give a real version of what happened."

"My way?" I laugh helplessly. "I was just playing around."

"We could, you know," murmurs Hye, the girl playing Johan Rule.

"We'd get in bad trouble, but it's not an excludable offense." Nim's voice rises like a kid's when promised a visit to the swimming hole.

What Nim is suggesting would be better than shutting down the production. It would be *reclaiming* the production. But it would likely be very, very costly.

"They could make it an excludable offense, though," says Ilo. "The nuns would be humiliated, and who *knows* what the viceroy would do? No one thought Sister Chlotilde would send Via to the workhouse just for mouthing off, did they?"

"If we don't do something, we'll be doing the production,

and I am *not* doing the production." Nim plants her rake like a banner. "If anyone has a better idea, now's the time. Otherwise, I'm following Malley's lead. I'm making up my own lines."

My mouth goes dry. I'm not going to help Loe keep secrets from people who have a lot to lose no matter what we decide to do. "Th-there *is* a plan. Loe and the honor girls are sabotaging the viceroy's throne with bad nails. It's going to collapse and—"

"What kind of stupid plan is that?" Nim cuts in. "The whole thing would wobble as the brute climbed up. He'd never agree to sit in it, especially considering how high it is. Would you?"

No. I wouldn't. Someone like the viceroy of New Weald definitely wouldn't.

"If it doesn't wobble, the nails aren't bad enough and the throne won't come down unless someone helps it along, and even then it might stay up. Whoever does the helping is done for, whether the throne actually collapses or not. Her chambermates, too." Nim narrows her eyes. "So much for no one getting caught."

Bringing down the viceroy sounded perfect. Too good to be true. I blink back tears. I did it again. I wanted to be an honor girl, so I did what would get me that instead of what was best for everyone. I should have thought it through, and now I've let these girls down.

"If we follow this so-called *plan*," Nim sneers, "one of

two things will happen. Either the throne is too wobbly and the nuns find the chief war criminal somewhere else to sit, or it's built securely enough to hold up his stupid rump during the production. Either way, *The Winning of New Weald* is back on. Starring us. Girls you promised wouldn't have to do it."

I can't look at them. Not when I'm about to cry. "I did promise. I meant it too. Other things are being sabotaged. I just need time to—"

"They're being slowed down," Hye says, "but that's about to end. Yesterday, the girls in the chamber next to mine got sent below when one of them who was in costuming splattered red dye on Johan Rule's cassock." She smiles faintly and tents the costume to show us. "Now he looks like he just came from committing a murder."

"Making up our own lines is the only way we can be sure the production won't happen," Ilo says in a low voice, and Hye nods grimly.

I swallow. They're both right. I promised, and I've completely failed to come up with a better plan.

"We've all got to agree," Nim says. "Each of us has to be willing to see the whole thing through, no matter what happens."

Like Tareliane and her chambermates. They also made a pact. They made it knowing what would happen. I cast around and manage, "If we—"

"You know what?" Ilo says. "Something good might

come of it. The viceroy is the emperor's brother, and the emperor is big on reforms. He might be willing to hear our side. He might think making Milean girls do this sort of production is cruel."

"Or maybe he'll think we're too stupid to learn lines," Nim adds. "He might figure the nuns gave us a task that was too hard for us."

"I'm in," Hye says, serious as a knife to the throat. After Nim, she easily has the worst part, and she says it like she's been waiting a long time for the chance. One by one the actors all agree to make up lines that tell a Milean story. Each time, my heart pounds a little harder, but these are girls who are standing up for themselves at last. I am finally not alone.

When it's my turn, I square up. Even though I know what's coming, I'm past the point where I can bring myself to comply. Even though I know what's coming, I tell them I'm in.

DAY 165

EXPANSION DAY STARTS WITH A NOVICE throwing open the door to chamber 10 and shaking each of us awake. We paid for the slow-down, mess-up approach last night when the nuns made everyone work well past the usual time for lights-out to get things finished, repaired, or otherwise production-worthy. It's nowhere near dawn when we stumble into the dining hall for breakfast, and the first- and second-rank girls are visibly outraged when there's nothing but oatmeal for everyone.

While we're eating, Sister Gunnhild paces the front of the room, worrying the ends of her veil. "The viceroy will be here promptly at ten, and this place must be perfect. After breakfast, you'll be dismissed to your production areas to prepare. Move quickly, and without any of this grumbling we've seen too much of lately."

My production area is the curtained-off space behind the stage where we're supposed to put on our costumes. Girls in all colors of scarves dragging their feet, asking to visit the wash station, accidentally-on-purpose forgetting their shoes in their rooms. The nuns and novices are the ones hurrying, rushing around the stage, checking that the big painted backdrops are ready to be hung in the right order, frantically laying out props.

The nuns have a lot riding on this production. This is their chance to prove what a good job they're doing. How the emperor was right to take a chance on them running the schools instead of appointing inquisitors and members of the nobility as teachers. Everything has to go perfectly today so the viceroy can report back to his brother the emperor and school can keep going along just as it is— Willa the brain-dead factory girl and scrubbing privies at the Cur estate and answering to our imperial names like all of this is normal somehow. Like it's never been any other way, and never should be.

I have to pass the viceroy's throne to get to my production area, and I shake my head sadly as I go by. Loe is going to be so disappointed when her plan fails, either when they reseat the viceroy or when the throne doesn't come down. Each time she gave me a batch of nails, I meant to tell her how her plan was flawed and the actors were going to reclaim the production instead, but then she'd hug me and whisper how glad she was that I was one of them now. All I could do was smile, even though it was hard to know how to feel. Now that I wasn't doing what she told me, I couldn't risk her trying to talk me out of it. Or worse, informing on us. But being hugged by the great-granddaughter of Everard Talshine was almost as nice as the ancestors' gentle hands on my head.

The actors are put to work helping the set builders uncoil and hook up hoses for the gas footlights until Sister Chlotilde, raving about the time, browbeats a harried Sister Gerta into releasing us so we can put on our costumes. In our production area, now a dressing room, the actors take off their uniforms and oh-so-slowly put on military coats and cassocks and filthy trousers. Nim levels a long glance at me as she buckles on Cav Horn's signature leather armor. I stall as long as I can before sliding into General Cur's awful graycoat. It's sweltering and heavy, dancing with those braided-string pigtails that still make me bellysick, and the only thing that keeps me from slinging it to the ground and stomping out of here is counting down the seconds till I can take it off and start giving my new lines.

I edge toward the curtain and peek out. The war criminals are seated in their viewing boxes, and the sides are draped with Embattled Crown tapestries and garlands of flowers that the costumers did their darnedest to ruin without seeming to.

"Sit here." Novice Lilac directs me impatiently toward

a battered stool. "I need to glue a false beard on your face. Nim, you too. Will you *hurry* with those boots?"

Jey told me the stagehands weren't able to convince Sister Gerta to let them dismantle and rebuild the throne. They had to make do with prying nails out and replacing them when her back was turned. Jey insisted I keep handing over the bad nails, even after she grudgingly admitted that Nim was probably right. *If it won't matter, let us do this. Let us know we did something.*

While Novice Bluebell mixes the glue, Novice Lilac moves behind me and starts grappling with my hair. I'm so surprised that I sit dead still for a long moment before I remember my plait is hidden there, on the underside.

"Hey!" I try to pull away. "Wait!"

"It's all right," Novice Lilac says, and there's a frown in her voice as she tries to pull all the flyaway strands and sections together. "I got special permission from Sister Gunnhild to pull it into a bun at the back of your neck. Just for the production, mind you."

"No! Stop!" It wouldn't be a real topknot, but after all these months it would be close enough, especially today. "Let me—!"

Novice Lilac's hands freeze. They freeze buried in the underside that she's just gathered into a handful with the rest. They freeze tangled in my plait.

Then she grips it tight, and with her other hand starts clawing the rest of my hair out of the way.

I should plead—*it's just a tangle, a bad knot, I should have sat under the dryer vent in the wash station instead of going to bed with it wet*—but it won't do any good. There's a breath of cold air on my neck, a chill I haven't felt in months. Not since I still had a topknot and all my ribbons dangled down. A brush of touch along my plait. Malliane's plait.

I can't breathe. I'm trembling all over. I am lost.

"Lilac! What's wrong with 1076?" Sister Chlotilde cranes her neck from where she's stitching a rip in Ilo's costume.

Novice Lilac spins me, pushes my loose hair up, and there's another tug on my plait. I brace for the crop. For the cursing and the screeching and the *ignorant dimwit, you'll be sorry now*. If I'm lucky, it'll make me numb for what's coming.

But Sister Chlotilde whistles low. Finally she says, "Well, then. Looks like this production's going to be more authentic than any of us thought."

The dressing room is behind the stage, and over my own shuddery breathing, I can hear Sister Gunnhild welcoming the viceroy and the other guests. Going on and on about Expansion Day and what a marvelous honor it is to celebrate our empire's glorious history, how we girls are delighted to share our small offering and hope it pleases.

I'm back in my uniform. They don't want the Hock Cur costume ruined. I'm holding my hair. One handful on either side of my face. It's silky from where I brushed it this morning. The same color as my da's. Sister Chlotilde sends Novice Peony to round up Jey and Pev and Mor. They'll face this same fate too, just like my first set of chambermates, who I dragged down with me. This is worse, though. Worse by tenscore.

It's not long before Novice Bluebell and Novice Lilac haul me off the stool and guide me out of the costuming area, down a short hallway made of blue draperies, and into the wings of the stage just as Sister Gunnhild is saying, ". . . consequences for an unfortunate decision, but which is ultimately what we do here at Forswelt, and at national schools across this great land."

The novices pull me stumbling onto the stage. It's nothing like rehearsal. Now there are people in the stands, lots of them, and garlands of flowers everywhere, and the viewing boxes lined with war criminals in their robes of state. The viceroy has his hand to his eyes like he's peering with interest, and I spot Maude Cur and that hateful Burgund Gaude, who even now lets his ponies wreck land my parents and grands and ancestors poured their lives into.

A chair appears and the novices shove me into it. Each holds one of my arms so firmly I don't bother to struggle.

"The mission of the national schools is to guide the New Wealdan people away from a barbarous past and help them find their place in the empire," Sister Gunnhild says. "We have simple, reasonable rules here. One is that there's no binding of the hair. What you are about to see will be shocking, but please remember that Kem made the conscious decision to break that rule. She will be the first, and her chambermates will share the same consequence in order of rank. The production will begin shortly after. Girls of Forswelt, take a warning from your classmate. We've created these guidelines for the sake of your future, and it is with solemn duty that we undertake this corrective measure for Kem's benefit. Bluebell?"

Novice Bluebell hands Sister Gunnhild a pair of shears much like the ones she shinked at me that first day at intake.

This is what it feels like to die by fire.

There's a tug on my head, then a grating *sniiip*. A handful of hair slithers down my arm. I blink and blink but it's no good. I'm sniffling and then sobbing and I can't even wipe away my tears because the novices are holding me tight. Another hank of hair, and another, bigger piece, because at least Sister Gunnhild isn't turning this into a sideshow. She snips quick and businesslike, right at the scalp, and there's no chunks of flesh torn out, no harsh burning. Not like how my parents were treated. Not like Jasperine or Everard. When she gets to my plait, she snicks it off clean and then slices it into small pieces one by one. I can't look anywhere but five feet in front of me, where the edge of the stage is lined with the clever little gaslight lamps I helped set up that are supposed to manage where the shadows fall, but are really making everything shiny-blurry and unreal.

I've lost my parents. I've lost my homestead. In a very short time I'll have lost the friendship of my three newly shorn chambermates, and likely every other girl in this school who so much as considered resisting. I've lost my hair and Malliane won't know me. I have no way to bind myself to her anymore. I have lost my whole family and now I have no one.

Novice Lilac pulls me out of the chair. I shuffle through my own hair. Someone rubs a towel over my tufty, bristly head. My scalp is cold, and my hand wants to reach up and feel but my brain is too scared of that. I stoop to grab handfuls of my hair—what for, I'm not sure—but Novice Bluebell is already pulling the soft tangles out of the way with a broom.

There's a clank and a rustle, the sound of tearing cloth, a drumming of feet and the clatter of things falling, Sister Gunnhild saying something like *What's the meaning of this?*

Somehow I'll have to face them. Every girl I made a promise to. Once the shearing is finished and everyone has said her lines. Once everyone from actors to costumers to stagehands has been prodded across the stage to take a bow while the viceroy and the war criminals politely clap for our little show.

The viewing platform hovers in the corner of my eye. Through my tears, through my rattling breath, through my bellysick, I catch sight of the viceroy. He's younger than I expected. Probably not yet thirty. He's grinning this faint, triumphant grin, like he's composing a report for the emperor in his head on how well the national schools are working, how children are learning that compliance brings reward and being ungovernable will only end in misfortune.

I'll give him misfortune. I'll give him *ungovernable*.

I leap off the stage and circle around toward the viceroy's throne. No one stops me. The crowd darts and hurries past me like show ponies once they've been spooked. The platform is taller up close, probably twelve feet high, the spindly legs painted royal purple and smelling faintly of cedar and riddled with nails that will snap like a neck.

After all this, I'll still have to play Hock Cur. The viceroy won't have a lick of sympathy for us now. He won't see the production as cruel. He'll think it's appropriate. He'll think it's *necessary*.

It won't matter, but I want to know I did something. I lift my heel and slam it hard against the throne's closest upright.

There's a deep, resonant crack, and the whole structure shudders. Someone in the war criminals' viewing box shouts, and even though my whole leg hurts like it's shattered, I kick the throne again. And again. And—

The slender upright folds in, and while I stand there nameless and alone, the platform caves and the viceroy slips and flails and falls.

It worked. Loe's plan. Jey and the stagehands got enough bad nails in. The viceroy of New Weald is plummeting rump over teakettle toward the ground. Halfway down, his leg catches one of the cross-braces and snaps—clear and wet like a carrot—then slithers loose from the brace. The viceroy lands in a dull clatter of limbs, bellowing like a dying cow.

That's when I start laughing. Every ancestor laughs with me, every last one who faced the pyre or the workhouse or the transport ship.

"You filthy crogen!" The viceroy gasps out each word. "You'll go to the workhouse for this! Every single one of you will *die* for this attack on my person! Everyone in this entire disobedient school!"

My ankle throbs. My knee, too. I can barely put weight on my whole left side. No one was going to get hurt or caught. If this was a song, I'd be bellowing the flying columns' battle cry and stabbing a fist in the air. It's not, though. Any moment now the novices will seize me. I'll go with them. Wherever they take me to wait for the wagon. It won't matter. A Milean might resist, but I'll never be Milean again.

I turn away from the viceroy writhing at my feet—and stop where I stand.

The stage is on fire.

Girls are everywhere, tearing down backdrops and soaking curtains with paint thinner and kicking over the footlights. Costumers, stagehands, prop girls, actors—they're streaming out of the dressing room and from backstage, grappling off their costumes and smashing tables and flinging burning rags everywhere. The war criminals are trapped in their viewing boxes, and nuns and novices are frantic, stumbling over their benches, shouting at the girls to line up by rank but also struggling to put out the fire and stop the wholesale destruction of the set.

Sister Gunnhild is trying to make her way through the crowd, toward the viceroy. "Your Grace, please. The guilty parties will be punished. I promise you we'll see to it."

That's me. She means me. I'm the one who kicked the throne. Unless she means that everyone who's not complying is now a guilty party.

Someone appears at my elbow. Nim, wearing just her undershift, like she's come right from the laundry. She must have ditched her Cav Horn outfit first thing. She's pale under her bright hair and staring, horrified, at the viceroy's leg, which is bent at two different angles it shouldn't be.

"Malley," she whispers, "what is this? What's happening?"

In a song, everything is bold and glorious. There's no shouting. No chaos. None of the bone-deep terror that comes from knowing what's going to happen to you and your friends at the end. Living through a songworthy act is nowhere near singing one.

Like dying.

The viceroy breathes through his teeth in tiny, grating wheezes. "Your parents. They're done too. Your brothers and sisters. Anyone you love. You hear me, girl?"

"You transported my parents," I growl down at him.

"They're already done, as far as the Crown's concerned."

He coughs a harsh laugh. "*Transported*. Your fool lot will believe anything."

My mouth opens. My heart judders.

Then I jerk my stick of drawing lead from my uniform pocket and jab it hard against the viceroy's throat. "Shut up. *Shut up*, you wretched pile of filth, or so help me I will *end* you."

"Back up! Leave him be!" Sister Gunnhild shouts. "Your Grace! Your Grace, how badly are you hurt?"

"We don't want any trouble!" Nim calls. "We're just—we're not doing the production. Not now, not ever!"

"The *what*?" Sister Gunnhild screeches. "Does it look like we could do the production now? You ungrateful wretches have ruined everything!"

I don't take my drawing lead from the viceroy's throat because he's *lying*, he has to be, because the Crown doesn't martyr Mileans anymore and there was a trial and a sentencing but oh shrines my ma and da boosted me up and out of the guardhouse and I never, *ever* saw them get on a transport ship.

"They didn't do anything." Nim's voice wavers. "The girls. You can't send us all to the workhouse. The newspapers—"

"I can," the viceroy rasps, "and I will."

Sister Gunnhild and Sister Gerta keep coming. So do the novices. Girls are flying past me, into the school and probably into hiding. Like that will save them somehow. Jey appears behind Nim and me. For a long moment, all I can see is her hair, unshorn and swishing down her back in a red-brown curtain. They didn't get to her. Then I realize she's pointing and signing frantically. The rest of the throne is tilting hard and dangerous. The whole thing's about to come down and we're going to be under it.

"Help me." I crouch and grab the viceroy under the armpits, then glance between Nim and Jey. "Please."

They do, reluctantly, and the three of us haul him still whimper-gasping up the trodden path and past the door with the complicated locks. As soon as we're through, I slam each of those locks closed one after another after another.

The sound echoes in the cavernous hall. The only other noise is the viceroy taking little hissing breaths.

We look at one another.

"What just happened?" Nim repeats, so quietly you can almost hear her signing along.

They're looking at me like I know, like I planned this somehow. I press both hands against my head. My bare, scruffy head. I muffle a sob.

"Malley?"

I'm not Malley anymore. I have no right to that name. I won't be Kem. But I don't know who I am now.

What happened? Jey grins. *What happened is that we just locked ourselves in the school with no nuns or novices. That means this place is ours now.*

No. What happened is I just signed the death warrant of every girl in this entryway who put hands on a royal person—an *injured* royal person—instead of letting the nuns help him. Maybe every girl at Forswelt.

"But . . . what do we *do*?" Nim asks, and she's looking everywhere but my head and it's all I can do not to cry.

I slide my scarred hands down my face. They're waiting. Nim and Jey. My friends. I was dead already, but they weren't. They could have rushed past me like the others, hidden out in their chambers, and braced for the aftermath. Maybe even lined up to inform on me.

Only here they are.

"I . . . um . . ." I flutter a hand, and when Jey nudges me pointedly, I use them both to sign. "We should figure out how many girls got inside and see if anyone's hurt. Make sure Jey's right and there are no nuns or novices in with us."

Jey nods and raises a hand to her forehead like the field captains in the flying columns once did. She disappears down the hall, and as she's rounding the corner, she pulls off her second-rank scarf and flings it to the floor.

Nim pads over to the viceroy and puts two fingers against his throat. "He's got a pulse, but it's slow. Creepy-slow. Also he's . . . passed out, I think. We have to do something about him."

"We let him rot," I reply.

"No. His leg is broken. Badly. If we don't set the break, he'll die. Shock or infection. It won't be pretty."

"Good."

"Malley, please." Nim sits back on her heels. "I get it. I do. But we're bad off right now, and a dead viceroy is trouble we do not want on top of that."

"You don't get it," I snap. "Your parents aren't dead. They weren't murdered by the Crown for—"

"My parents dumped me here on the first day this place opened," Nim cuts in, low and fierce. "Me and my Cav Horn hair. Only twelve people beat them to it, and they got out of paying the rent for a whole season as a bonus. Don't feel too bad. It was better than living in the shed all alone, like I'd done something wrong just being born."

The entranceway goes quiet. Even though someone— probably a nun or novice—is pounding on the door outside and shouting.

My ma made my hammock out of crib blankets. She stitched them together by the dim glow of our cook fire after putting all her daylight hours into the croplands. My da roasted my breakfast millet each morning even though it took way longer than boiling, just because he knew I liked it that way best. I miss my parents every day, but it's something knowing they miss me too, and if they really aren't alive anymore, that they missed me every moment they were.

"The Crown doesn't martyr Mileans anymore," Nim says softly. "The viceroy was trying to get to you. It worked."

The viceroy lies crumpled like a wad of chewed-up

paper, his embroidered waistcoat filthy and his leggings stained red where bone shards have cut through. He knows there's no way I'll ever know if he's lying. Whether my ma and da really are sweating their guts out in the penal colony, miserable but alive, or rotting in some shallow burial trench.

"We need an imperial pardon," Nim says, and her voice is sturdy again, her war face back on. "That's the only thing that will save us now. Us and the nuns. If the viceroy dies, there's no hope at all."

If he dies, I will smile, just like my ma when she heard the charges read in court. But Nim's right. As long as his brother is alive, the emperor might be persuaded to grant us a pardon, and that will save every girl at Forswelt, even the ones who just wrecked the stage. I turn away, muttering swears in Milean, but there's no one to give me demerits for speaking an outlawed tongue, so I shout those swears. I shout them long and loud, but finally I pull myself together and rasp, "I don't know how to set a bone. Do you?"

"Yeah." Nim flinches like she learned the hard way. "Let's take him to the infirmary."

Nim brings a stretcher, but after I help carry the viceroy into the tidy whitewashed room and heave him onto one of the beds, I turn on my heel and storm into the corridor. Just because this pile of filth will die without medical treatment doesn't mean I have be the one to give it to him. I crouch and lean against the wall. My bare scalp scrapes cold stone, and stupid tears slip out.

I should turn myself in. Open those locks and surrender to the nuns. If I could be sure they wouldn't punish anyone else, I'd do it, but that's not how things work at Forswelt. I don't know how long I've sat there when Jey taps my shoulder, sits down beside me, and says, *I went through the whole school. Everyone was out watching the production. There are no nuns or novices anywhere inside. Just girls.*

I nod blearily. I should be happier. But my leg is aching and my tufty head is cold and I have no name and no family.

They got the fire put out, finally, Jey goes on. *There's no stage anymore. Just charred timbers and shreds of canvas. It's the best thing you're going to see all day. If you want, we can go to the roof and you can have a look for yourself.* She grins and jiggles a gold spyglass on a chain around her neck that must have once belonged to a nun.

"I can't," I whisper, and it's as hard to say as it is to sign. *Just . . . you do it, all right?*

Do what? Jey peers at me. *You're not losing your guts for this now, are you? Malley—*

"I'm not Malley anymore! I'm not anything!" I slump against the wall and whisper, "Not even Milean. Not after . . . what happened."

Jey narrows her eyes. I flinch because I spoke aloud and reading lips is hard and she's right to be angry, but instead she says, *What happened? What happened was every girl at Forswelt rushing the stage and setting it on fire after what the nuns did to you. Tearing apart their costumes. Pulling down sets. Because you were the one who told them they could resist. You were the one who gave them hope.*

Like a song. Like every song that starts running through my head, and maybe I haven't lost everything. Not if I still have the songs.

Not gonna lie, Jey says. *You are one bald girl, but Malliane's going to know you. I'm not sure how. I just know she will. Because that look you had? Pressing a sharp stick to the viceroy's throat? Not caring what came next? That's the most Milean thing I think I've ever seen. Something right out of "Everard's Flying Column."*

I want to believe her. I want to believe I'm still Milean and capable of songworthy acts, because maybe if I've done something songworthy, I can do it again. My name-kin may have turned away from me, but it just might be possible to convince her to turn back.

Sooner or later the nuns will find a way in here. Sister Gunnhild must carry a key, or there's one kept elsewhere, maybe in the provincial capital. There might be a secret entrance none of us knows about. Once they're back in charge, the nuns will appeal to the emperor and explain how we plotted and schemed to ruin the production and attack the viceroy, how there's no hope for us and everyone knows where ungovernable girls must be sent if they can be of no use to the empire any other way.

Nim asked what's happening. What this is. It's our last

few minutes—hours—days—on this earth. I'm not going to spend any of it a New Wealdan.

I strip off my uniform and put it back on inside out. I fling my stupid orange scarf into the corner, then head straight for the service ramps that lead below. I sent three innocent girls down there because I thought my way was the only way, so it's right that the first thing I do is get them out. The rest of the school was made to attend the production, but as far as the nuns are concerned, no one below even exists.

The laundry door is locked. Zoh has a key—I've seen it around her neck, outlined under her uniform—and any other one is likely outside with the nuns. I hammer a fist on the door and then rattle it, hoping to lure Zoh to open up, but she clearly knows better. Cursing, I wind through the hallways till a cracked-open door makes me stop and backtrack. It's a cozy little chamber painted pale blue, and there's a plushy padded chair in front of a funnel-shaped amplifier set into the wall. The observation room. It has to be. This is where a novice recites chapel prayers all day so girls in correction have no choice but to listen to blah-blah *obedience* and blah-blah *compliance*.

This is the best I'm going to do without a key. It's up to the girls below to finish the job. I drop into the chair and pull the funnel close. "Girls of Forswelt! A flying column of Mileans has wrecked the nuns' stupid production and locked every last one of them outside the building.

Sister Gunnhild's not in charge anymore. Jasperine Vesley is running this place now, and I'm liberating the workhouse underneath this excuse for a school in her name. As of right now, there are no demerits. No ranks. No freaking numbers. As of right now, you aren't in Forswelt National School anymore. You are in Milea. This is *Free Milea*."

I head back to the laundry and put my ear against the door. I want to say I hear a commotion, but it could also be cart wheels against bare floor stones. I've done all I can for them now, so I go up the ramps again and liberate everyone else.

I start in the residence wing. I go chamber by chamber, banging on doors. Girls are sitting on their beds or hiding under them. They're gathered with chambermates in the dining hall. They're tense and fidgety, and their eyes go from my sheared head to my scarred hands to my inside-out uniform like I'm some kind of ghost.

I say it in Milean again and again. Jasperine Vesley is in charge now. No more ranks. No more numbers or imperial names. Toss your scarves. This is Free Milea.

Some girls follow me, tentatively peering into the corridor and glancing both ways like they're sure this is a trick and they'll be given demerits even after everything that happened today. Others leave their rooms boldly and fan out through the school, flinging scarves as they go. They know exactly what this means.

Forswelt belongs to us now.

It's strange to walk through the halls in broad daylight and go where I want. I've never done that here. Only along deer paths and in fields and down the long, sloping bank of my homestead. I search a few classrooms for girls in hiding, but they've all been trashed and there's nothing to crouch behind. Tables have been overturned and kicked to pieces. Books are strewn across the floors, pages torn and fluttering everywhere. Someone has drawn a life-size picture on the wall of a nun with x-ed-out eyes swaying from a hanging tree.

I stop in the doorway of classroom 8. Somewhere in this wreckage is my primer, torn to pieces. My last link with my mystery friend, each of us working on pictures, each knowing the other was seeing them. Lost now, like so many other things. I duck out of the room and walk away, scrubbing a wrist over my eyes because the one thing I am not going to do in Free Milea is cry.

I walk through the entire school twice. I can't sit still. I check cupboards and closets for nuns and novices and girls who haven't heard the news. I end up back at the front entrance, running my hands over those three complicated locks. There are only two doors that lead outside, and both are secured this way. I know, because I spent my first two weeks here checking. This door is meant to keep us in, but now it's keeping the nuns out.

It can't work forever.

There's a burst of sustained pounding on the door, then a muffled shout of "Girls! You will open this door immediately!"

It's Sister Chlotilde, and the rage in her voice is pulsing through the wood and stone, but there's an edge of fear as well. Students in her school not only insulted the dignity of the Crown, but broke its leg and took it hostage. The nuns need that imperial pardon as much as we do, and even if he grants it, the emperor might not let any of them keep their jobs.

I can't resist. I beat on the door until she's quiet, and then I call, "Why should we? You worried about something?"

"1076? Is that you? Blast it, I should have known."

That's what Burgund Gaude said on the witness stand when the Crown prosecutor called him to testify. That my ma never looked him in the feet when he rode past. My da never smiled when handing over our land dues. Lord Gaude should have known they were planning something. Ingratitude was written all over them plainly.

"You will open the door right now. How dare you behave in this barbarous, unscrupulous way?"

"The viceroy is still alive," I shout. "We're treating his injury. Barbarous and unscrupulous would have been leaving him to be crushed by the platform. Even though he deserves a whole lot worse."

"The viceroy's injury is too serious for you dimwits to treat," Sister Chlotilde says sternly. "Open the door so we can provide him with proper medical attention."

I touch the three complicated locks. If the nuns could force them somehow, or if they had a key, or if they planned to batter down the door, they'd be doing it now. If they're demanding that we let them in, it means they can't get in any other way. It means we're safe.

It means we're free.

"If you want us to open the door," I reply, "you'll have to make it worth our while."

"You're making *demands*? You don't get to make demands!" Sister Chlotilde's tirade devolves into threats and blustering, so I walk away. Chin up, limping from where I kicked the viceroy's throne, and grinning so hard my face hurts. The nuns and novices will just have to amuse themselves giving demerits to one another for a while.

Nim wanted to know what we're going to do. I don't know about her, but I'm going to do whatever I want. I can go where I like now. Anywhere in Forswelt. So I do.

The nuns' private quarters are a lot like ours, only they each get a room to themselves. Same with the novices. Somehow I expected fluffy carpets and beautiful wall hangings and thick, comfortable piles of blankets. But it's the same white walls and wooden bed frames. Same flagstones in their private wash station, same showerheads and sinks.

Their dining room is nicer than ours, though, and there's a cake on a stand under a glass dome. I smear the cake across the counter, then smash the glass cover against the flagstones. It shatters in the most satisfying way, so I go to the nearest table and fling the cutlery and scatter the chairs and send the table flying. Then I storm to the next one and the next, till the whole dining room is in ruins.

I've wanted to do something like this since I got here, but it doesn't feel nearly as good as I thought it would. I pick up a chair and set it on its legs and sit down. Put my head in my hands. My stubbly, bristly head in my scarred, blistery hands. This is what I get for chasing the songworthy thing instead of doing what's best for everyone. I should have backed away from the viceroy and let the nuns help him.

Except he was about to send us all to the workhouse. Maybe I saved everyone by pulling him inside the school. I didn't take him hostage on purpose, but if I hadn't, the emperor would have no reason to offer us a pardon. Now we have something they want.

I pull my drawing lead out of my pocket and rub a thumb over its point. I could have ended the viceroy there in the mud. I wanted to. Jey was right—I didn't care what came next. Something stopped me, though, and it wasn't feeling sorry for an injured man or worry for my chambermates.

"Malliane," I whisper, but then I choke because she's gone and I am worse than alone. Things hurt when they matter, but they also hurt when nothing matters.

I slide the lead stick back into my uniform pocket, and my knuckles brush something soft and tickly. The tiny plait. Carefully traded from gown to gown each morning when I get dressed. I pull it out and hold it in both hands. Hairs are fraying off the sides, but it's still tightly bound through the middle. Still tethered firm at either end.

A song starts running through my head, only it's not any song I know. It's a song about a little braid and a bigger braid and all the ways a girl can be Milean. The words happen together in my head like they've always been there, like it really could be possible that we're all schoolmasters now. I'm hunched over in the chair, holding tight to my plait with both hands, when the ghost of a warm but gentle weight falls on my stubbly head. Like a blessing, maybe, if I still thought something like that was possible.

"Hey."

I reel around in the rump-bruising chair. "Fee!" I'm up and across the room and hugging her fierce and sure, but she's sharp and bony under her inside-out uniform. She's got a bowl of greens under her arm, and her pockets are full of mushrooms.

"Where did you get actual food?"

"Dining hall," she replies, taking a bite from a tomato. "Girls from the kitchen brought up the dishes they made for the viceroy's banquet. Everyone's there now, eating like they've never seen vegetables before."

"So the girls in janitorial heard me on the speaker?" I ask. "You got your prefect to let you out?"

"If by *let*, you mean girls held her down and took the key off her neck, then yes." Fee doesn't sound proud or defiant like I would if I'd done that to Zoh. Instead she sounds like she could sleep for a year. Then she adds in a faint, scratchy voice, "I guess I should be angrier. You up to your old tricks. But I wouldn't be out of that place otherwise."

"My old tricks?" I echo, but I know what she means, and although I'm itching to defend myself—to tell her how the throne plan was Loe's, that girls were already sabotaging things left and right before I said a word, and the most dangerous thing we planned we didn't even get to do—I don't. I have to earn Fee's trust. So I say, "This is Free Milea, but it's not mine. It's *ours*. We're going to sing outlawed songs and recite the Roll of Honor and plait our hair and be Milean."

Fee nods slow and deliberate, like those months of bending and scrubbing taught her to make every movement count. "Then what?"

I frown, and Fee goes on, "Girls are celebrating in the dining hall. No one's wearing a uniform, and everyone I saw had thrown away her scarf and plaited her hair. But what's going to happen when it's over?"

She hands me a folded piece of paper. I take it and read aloud, "'To the girl who finds this note. If you open the door now and let us in, you won't be punished with the rest. If someone is reading it to you, neither of you will be punished.'"

"The nuns will keep slipping notes under the door till one of us takes them up on it," Fee says. "Sooner or later, someone will."

We haven't been free long enough to trust that anything will come of standing together. The only evidence that Mileans didn't just knuckle under and comply is in songs we've been forbidden to sing and old days that were too costly to think on that much.

I refold the note into a tight packet. I very much want to be free.

"This is something everyone should see." I hold out the note, but Fee shakes her head and disappears into one of the nuns' private chambers with her food.

I make myself walk toward the dining hall. I don't get to tell Free Mileans what they can and can't do, especially not Fee. I'm rounding a corner when I bump into Loe. She's plaited her hair and wound it into an elegant topknot. Like hair should look. Like I haven't seen in months, not since the judge read the sentence and my ma's glorious pile of braids shone in the gaslight for the very last time.

Like my hair will never look again.

Loe folds her arms, harsh like a graycoat cinching a bandolier, and says coldly, "I should congratulate you. Apparently your plan to sabotage the production went off without a hitch. Especially toppling the viceroy's throne. That idea of yours was clearly genius."

"I tried to tell them—"

"I really don't think you did!" Loe barks, but then she lets out a long, shuddery breath. "There's steel in you, though. I'll give you that. Somehow you've got Roll of Honor guts when none of your grands or ancestors were anywhere near it. Just your ma and da come close, and their pointless little spree was barely worth noting." She peers at me. "I could never have done what you did. I mean, what if they hadn't reacted like that? They could just as easily have sat there being glad it wasn't them."

She means the other girls. The ordinary girls. That's Jey she's running down. Pev and Mor. Nim.

Loe thinks I plaited my hair and got caught that way on purpose.

"It was a huge risk, setting yourself up as a martyr like that. But now that it's done, now that we're in charge, we've got work to do." Loe grabs my wrist and pulls me down the corridor, talking over her shoulder. "We've taken over two chambers side by side and there's an extra bed. You'll stay with us. Easier to plan that way. Easier to keep this going in the direction we want."

She's talking like I have a topknot as sleek and pretty as hers. Like I'm someone with enough Roll of Honor guts to be a martyr.

Fee appears at the top of the corridor, holding her bowl of greens against her hip. I wave her over, but her attention is on Loe and she doesn't move.

"Koa's got that one—Triesteline, I should say." Loe

points to the bed against the far wall, which is defiantly rumpled and not perfectly made for inspection. "You can have either of these in the middle. That one's mine."

I'm still in the doorway. The great-granddaughter of Everard Talshine is waiting for me to join her. She'd have me take a bed next to the descendants of men and women whose stories and songs I've known since I was small. They would invite the daughter of Pirine and Vinnio to step over their threshold and closer to the Roll of Honor. It's all but saying I've done songworthy acts, and so have my ma and da.

Only I'm still in the doorway. Songs running through my head. "I don't know that there's anything to plan." Considering I'm the child of people who did something barely worth noting. "I'll be sharing with Nim and Jey. Fee, too. If she'll have me as a chambermate again."

Fee takes a small step closer to me.

"Oh. Those girls." Loe smiles politely. "If you're sure."

Jasperine would plan. She'd have girls keeping watch and gathering supplies and setting trip wires so they'd know if graycoats were trying to sneak up on them. Only I don't want to do any of that. I've had enough of someone telling us where to be and what to think. The girls can find the kitchens if they're hungry. They can start a hedge school or wreck a classroom or stare at a blank wall. They can sleep in a room all alone or on a table in the dining hall or hang a hammock like I plan to do. I'm not about to tell a

Free Milean where she can go or what she has to do.

That is what Jasperine would have done, if there was any way she could have.

"Yes. I'm sure." I smile at Loe, no hard feelings, and then I rejoin Fee, the corners of the folded note poking my palm. I make the mistake of looking over my shoulder, though, and Loe's studying me from her bed with narrowed eyes, like she can't believe she heard me right.

In the dining hall, Pev is standing on a table, singing "The Inquisitor and the Goat," though it's more shouting than melody. The gaslight glints off her piled plaits already threaded through with makeshift ribbons. The nuns didn't find her in time either.

All at once I feel lighter, despite the note in my hand.

When she's done, I climb onto a table and wave a hand for attention. The girls sitting there make that field-captain gesture. I don't know what to say to that—we might be a flying column, but no one's been elected commander—so I hold up the note and raise my voice. "The nuns shoved this under the front door. It says whoever lets them in won't be punished with the rest of us."

The excited murmur of chatter dies instantly.

"I'll hand this to whoever wants to take them up on it," I say. "Right now. In front of everyone."

"That's not fair."

Heads swivel toward the back of the room, and people

step away from the girl who spoke. It's Mor, my chamber-mate. Her hair is plaited and piled too, and even though I'm glad to see it, I can't help but run a hand over my bristly scalp. She's standing chin-up and brave, even though girls near her are glaring and muttering what have to be bad words.

"Stop, stop." I gesture for quiet and mostly get it. "Let her talk."

"It's not fair," Mor repeats. "I didn't want to do the production. I did my share of sabotage. Ask anyone assigned to set creation. But locking the nuns out? Taking the viceroy hostage? I don't want to go to the workhouse, Malley. It's not fair for you to decide this for us."

"Why are you here, then?" Loe sweeps into the dining hall, Koa behind her. "No one made you run into the school when everything went to pieces. Knuckle-unders should have stayed outside with the nuns."

A lot of girls didn't make it back into the school. Or they decided not to try. Jey told me a handful of nuns escorted them in the direction of the Cur estate in long lines, as if they were going to vocational training. She saw them from the roof, where she's been keeping an eye on the nuns and novices who are still out front, milling in confusion like show ponies when the pasture gate is open. Either the nuns are worried that the other girls will change their minds and make trouble if they stay nearby, or those girls are already bound for the workhouse just for wrecking the production.

I hiss at Loe, then call for quiet again. This time it's harder. "You're right. It's not fair, and I don't want to go to the workhouse either. That's why I'm here with this note. That's why I didn't rip it up and not tell people about it." I swallow hard. "I'm here so we can vote. Like our ancestors did. We have to vote on what to do."

A murmur runs through the room. We all know about the vote. No one's ever seen one, though. No one still alive, anyway.

"The way I see it, we have two choices," I go on. "We can negotiate or we can hold out."

"You can't negotiate with Wealdans!" a girl shouts.

"Ask the Hanged Maidens how well that worked. Oh wait, you can't!" growls another.

"The Hanged Maidens didn't have the viceroy of New Weald doped up with opium and tied to a bed in the infirmary," Nim says, calm but loud enough to carry over the chatter. Her plaits are piled like everyone else's, but they're not in any name-kin pattern. Just simple three-strand braids. That can't be right, though. Surely Nim's parents gave her a *name*.

"The only way any of us are walking out that door is if the emperor gives us an imperial pardon," Loe says. "We have to trade the viceroy's life for ours."

"Some life," mutters a girl near me, and another grunts in disgust. They're right. We're not meant to live. Not as Mileans. We're meant to survive as New Wealdans.

I was a thumbnail from opening the viceroy's throat with my drawing lead. This must be why I didn't. If I still had name-kin, I'd think it was Malliane who whispered in my ear to stay my hand.

If the nuns and the emperor want the viceroy back in one piece, they'll have to make things a whole lot better for us. There'll be no repealing the Education Act. No shuttering the national schools and sending us home to our parents—those of us who still have parents. But there's no reason we have to be ranked and compete for privileges. No reason we have to wear uniforms with the imperial crest. No reason we have to be set apart by scarves and given demerits willy-nilly. No reason they have to feed us bread when they know it will make us grainsick and there's no shortage of vegetables.

Mor is near tears. "This is going to get us all sent to the workhouse!"

Jey starts signing, and I shout what she's saying so the whole room can hear. "Jey says there's no way that will happen. Something that catastrophic will make the Education Act look like a big mistake after the emperor has made reform the centerpiece of his reign. Ordinary Wealdans don't want their taxes spent coddling us, and the nobility still think they should be running the schools, since they own the factories we're sent to and the boardinghouses we're made to live in and the shops that take the special money we're paid with. The emperor has to make reform successful, and dozens of detention wagons rolling out of Forswelt will not look successful. He won't punish all of us."

"So he'll only punish some of us?" Nim raises a mocking eyebrow. "Are you volunteering?"

"No! Maybe. If I have to. But it won't come to that. Not when we have something they want at any price. All we've got to do is hold together. All of us. Like a flying column. This is Free Milea, remember?" I jump off the table and walk more purposefully through the room than I feel. Girls pull back as I go, and soon I'm in front of Mor and I hold out the note. "Here. Take it. If you honestly believe I'm trying to get you killed—here."

Mor shakes her head slow and folds her arms. I hold the note out to her for a full five seconds, then swing my hand above my head. "Anyone else? Now's your chance. Turn us in and save yourself. If you trust the goodwill of the Wealdan servants of the Nameless God who demanded that you put on a production about the conquest of your homeland to celebrate that occasion."

I hold my breath, but no one says a word. Not a single girl in the whole room.

"Right." I climb back onto a table. "Like I said, we vote. Like the flying columns did. Like free Mileans did. Loe's made a proposal. Do we negotiate?"

Girls around the room start sitting on the floor. One by one, like we learned in hedge school was how our ancestors decided things. Sitting meant you agreed with what the speaker was saying, and standing meant you wanted to dissent. Soon, Mor is the only person on her feet. She keeps shaking her head, polite but deliberate.

"C'mon, just agree," Loe snaps. "My great-grandda was Everard Talshine! I wouldn't have proposed negotiating if it wasn't a good idea."

"No one's making you do anything—Gracienne," I say, as Mor looks away and the pattern of her plaits ripples under the gaslight. "If you're with us, it's got to be because you want to be."

Mor presses a hand to her forehead, then says, "I'll agree if you're the one to negotiate."

"What?" Loe shouts. "No way! It was my idea! I'll be the one to do it."

"We vote," Fee replies firmly. "Like our ancestors did."

I grin. I can't help it. But Loe's face is red and she's studying the ground in fierce, proud humiliation. This isn't going to work if we let the ranks and scarves get in our heads and keep us at one another's throats. It's not going to work if there's no way for Loe to save face.

So I say, "Both of us will go. That is, I propose that Loe and I both negotiate. Along with Fee and Nim and Jey. So no one has to be alone up there."

"No thanks," Fee mutters, and at same time Loe says, "Koa should come too."

Not a single girl stands up to dissent. I smile at Koa so she knows I don't object, but it seems silly to care about honor girls and ordinary girls at this point. We're all Mileans, and we're all in this together.

At length the room grows quiet. It's one thing to say we're in Free Milea. Quite another to do something this Milean. Something right out of the hedge schools that kept these things alive and vivid over three generations.

We can't just negotiate for a pardon. We won't have this chance again. We have to ask for more.

Jey shows us a room off Sister Gunnhild's office where we can get to the maintenance ladders that lead to the roof. Songs are running through my head already. No Milean has ever been in a position to negotiate with Wealdans with any chance of success. Not Everard. Not anyone. We can get extra concessions. These girls are just not thinking big enough.

One by one, we climb through the narrow, dark shafts and step onto the shingles. The roof is peaky, and we have to crawl carefully across until we get to the side that overlooks the courtyard. The only sign of the stage is a wide square of blackened ground and a neat pile of charred timber. Everything else that could hint at the production is gone. Even the postholes from the throne and viewing boxes have been filled in. I should have come up here when Jey suggested it and seen the ruins for myself. The yard is too tidy now, too ordered, as if a lack of wreckage means the riot never happened.

Nuns and novices stand in clusters, glancing at the school like they're still not quite sure what happened. There are no girls anywhere, and I hope they're all at the Cur estate being kept away from our bad influence and not somewhere worse. We find spots along the edge of the roof, perched on ledges or holding downspouts for balance. Jey leans back against the shingles, her gold spyglass at the ready. When they see us, Sister Gunnhild and Sister Chlotilde move closer, onto the pebbled pathway that leads to the front door.

I lean out as far as my grip will allow. "We're here to negotiate the viceroy's release."

"Right now he's in the infirmary, but he's in bad shape," Nim adds, signing for Jey's benefit. "We only found three bottles of opium. It's not going to keep him sedated long."

Sister Gunnhild fidgets with her riding crop in small, menacing swishes, but she calls up calmly, "Very well. What do you have in mind?"

"We want an imperial pardon for every girl in school," Loe shouts.

"After what you traitors did?" Sister Chlotilde laughs, harsh and incredulous. "You can't ask for that."

I giggle. I think we can, and I think it's not the only thing we can ask for, but I'm not going to speak for everyone before they've had a chance to vote on what those things might be.

"A full pardon for everyone is the only thing that will get the viceroy out of here," Koa adds.

Sister Chlotilde leans toward Sister Gunnhild and says something, but she's too far away for me to hear.

"Very well, an imperial pardon," Sister Gunnhild calls up. "You have it. Now let us in at once."

Loe starts to stand, but Jey lowers her stolen spyglass, tugs her down, and says, *Hold on. Sister Chlotilde just said something about promising us anything so long as it gets us to open the door.* I turn to Jey, bewildered, and she gestures at the nuns in disgust. She's told me before how hard it is to read lips, but she's clearly suspicious enough to be ready for something like this.

"Sister Gunnhild doesn't have the authority to promise us a pardon," Nim breathes. "How can we believe anything she tells us?"

When none of us respond to the promise of a pardon, the nuns start arguing. Jey cackles, the spyglass back at her eye, every few moments letting it hang on its chain around her neck while she fills us in. *Sister Gunnhild just told Sister Chlotilde something about how she didn't think we were buying it. She's mad because she spoke too quickly and blew her chances of tricking us. She must really think we're stupid. Oh! Now Sister Chlotilde is blaming Sister Gunnhild for doing something* she *suggested!*

"What I meant to say was that I will do my best to convince the emperor that you girls should have a pardon," Sister Gunnhild finally shouts, "but I shouldn't have promised it to you. I'll summon an imperial emissary who can speak on the emperor's behalf. It'll take several days for him to get here from the provincial capital, though, and by then it may be too late for the viceroy. If you allow the doctor in to see what she can do for him, it will go a long way toward convincing the emperor that this whole incident is just a misunderstanding that got out of control. A misstep. That's all."

Sister Chlotilde is saying how she'll give us a misstep. Jey's not smiling anymore. *If it were up to her, she'd bring back the pyre.*

Everard must have stood where I am now. I have things he didn't have, though. I lean out and call, "We'll have an answer for you once we've had a chance to vote on it."

"You'll *vote* on it?" Sister Gunnhild's reasonable expression shatters. "You don't get to vote! Your lot is not capable of governing yourselves. Your role is to *obey*."

Loe laughs aloud. "Oh, really? Then we might not be capable of letting the doctor in."

The nuns start blustering like wind through gaps in the shingles, and I turn toward the maintenance ladders, the others behind me in a row. When we're back in Sister Gunnhild's office, I lean against her desk, grinning. "They did not like the word *vote*, did they?"

"She'll send for the emissary, though." Koa belatedly remembers to sign as she speaks. "No way are any of the nuns going to risk their own necks."

But will Sister Gunnhild actually try to convince him to get us a pardon as well? Jey asks. *I don't think we can trust her.*

"Of course we can't." Loe scowls. "We have to trust that the emperor loves his brother as much as the newspapers say."

I turn to Nim. "Is the viceroy going to die in the next few days?"

"I doubt it. He's not in the best shape, but we're giving him a lot of opium, and now he just sleeps." Nim smiles. "I may have lied about how many vials we have."

I grin, first at her and then at the others who are not quite standing near her.

Loe nods. "So it's not like we have to let in the doctor. We'll take a vote because we said we would. I have no plans to jump to do a Wealdan's bidding, though."

"We'll vote tomorrow, then," Koa says. "Are we agreed? We make the nuns wait. We make them take us seriously."

Maybe the next day, Jey replies with a scowl. *I don't know about you, but I'm in no hurry to go back to the way things were.*

"Then we shouldn't," I say, brightening, but Loe pushes open the dining hall's double doors, and she and Koa shove into the room ahead of us. It doesn't look like anyone has gone to bed. These girls are murmuring, anxious and confused. This is not the time to take another vote, no matter how much I want us all to have a chance at better conditions. There will be time tomorrow to convince them. So I pull in a deep breath and announce, "The nuns are bringing in someone from the imperial court to discuss a pardon. No promises, though—"

The rest is drowned by a massive wave of clapping and cheering and hooting and whistling and stomping and chanting *"Mal-li-ane,"* like it's still my name somehow. Like maybe I'm not alone and forgotten after all.

DAY 1 OF FREE MILEA

I WAKE UP SORE TO THE BONES OF MY BONES, and my face hurts where it was pressed against something unforgiving. I'm on the floor in the dining hall. There are lines from the planks pinched into my cheeks and chin.

I didn't sleep in a bed last night.

We are still free.

Gaddy is seated at a table nearby, eating a big bowl of turnips and onions. She's wearing a shirt and trousers dyed a vivid turquoise. Emmy is at Gaddy's table in her under-shift, busily stitching a length of pink cloth. When she turns her work, I realize it used to be a uniform. Gaddy sees me awake and waves me over. She's having hedge school soon, and she'd like me to be there. The girls who came up from below have heard some wild rumors about the production—Were the costumes really covered with false pigtails? Did the nuns really make someone recite the conversion doctrine?—and she'd have me give the whole story as a lesson. I agree, because even thinking about that stage on fire, girls everywhere tearing it down, makes words come together in my head like pieces of a song.

I stuff myself with carrots and celery, then go with them to classroom 8. My heart hurts just standing in the doorway, but I walk in anyway, toward the circle of girls sitting on the floor. The room has been cleaned up somewhat. The tables have been stacked in the corners and loose papers pushed aside. There's a space by the bookshelf. Just being near where my primer was will have to be enough.

I'm about to sit down when I catch sight of bold, angular pencil strokes in a book lying open on top of the shelf. *N is for National School,* with the school on fire like I'd drawn disaster into being.

It's my primer. Whole. I swipe it up and fly through the pictures one at a time. She found it. She saved it, and she left it here for me to find, with a new picture-message. Holding this book, turning the pages like each is a miracle, makes me feel the smallest bit songworthy. The smallest bit Milean.

There's a new picture. *G is for Graycoat,* only now it's *G is for Girls,* and a crowd of Milean girls are burying long knives into the soldier that gave me the shudders on my first day in class. The girls are sure and fierce, and they look a lot like Loe and Jey and Koa and Fee and Nim and me, girls who would ordinarily never be drawn together under any circumstances.

I'll have to add another picture and bring it back for her. Maybe *U is for Ungovernable*. There'll be a door with three locks, girls singing outlawed songs late into the night, eating vegetables and wearing what used to be uniforms restitched into shirts and trousers.

Once Gaddy's hedge school wraps up, she and Emmy show me where their new clothes came from. Some girls from the laundry have taken over the nuns' sitting room, and now it's a workshop. Against the far wall, there's a bathtub trailing broken pipes that has been dragged from some nun's private bathroom. It's full of bluing that's bleaching the Embattled Crown off the front of uniforms so they can be dyed yellow and aquamarine and deep, radiant purple. Colors never tied to a rank. Gowns flutter like battle banners from chairbacks and coat hooks, dripping dry, ruining the shiny hardwood floor. The walls and furniture are streaked and daubed and spattered with dye. It's like being inside a rainbow. Girls are laughing, sorting through the piles of bright clothes for a color they like, and there's a giggling sewing circle taking place on the couches.

In all the months I've been at national school, I've never heard girls laugh like this. Open and honest and free, like there's something worth celebrating. Something worth enjoying. I spend the whole day in the makeshift work-shop, cutting wool and sharpening scissors and mixing dye and threading needles and making ribbons of the scraps, because it's the first time in ages that I thought of home without wanting to cry.

As it gets late, we gather in the room we once used for free time, where people have apparently spent the whole day kicking down the room dividers. I sit in the corner, my primer across my knees open to *F is for Factory*. F is also for Flying Column. In this case, it's a flying column burn-ing down a factory. The picture is my best one so far, and it always makes me smile. I turn the page to *H is for Horse*, but H is really for Homestead. I start drawing them in the background behind the huge horse and its big stupid smile. A row of homesteads, each with a kitchen garden and back-ing to the croplands we worked with our neighbors.

It used to be all I wanted. A homestead with a snug hearth and a root cellar full to bursting with everything the garden could bring up. It was once the most Milean thing I could think of. But then it was gone. Quietly, casually, with the stroke of a pen somewhere across the sea in some white-marbled imperial chamber, because happy show ponies need plenty of land to stretch their stubby legs. Gone beyond reckoning, but not before taking my parents with it.

I turn pages till I get to *S is for Summer*. A while ago my mystery friend began to draw *S is for Schoolmaster*. Her careful, bold lines suggest shoulders and a long traveling cloak, but the face and topknot are still unfinished. I rough in Master Grenallan's unruly pigtails, his thrice-patched trousers. His wild eyebrows and sad, faraway stare.

Master Grenallan was one of the last schoolmasters, which was why he couldn't stay near Trelawney Crossing all the time. "Other kids, other kids," he would mutter, "so many little babies," and away he'd go with his rucksack on his back, barefoot and bareheaded, to places we weren't told about so we couldn't be made to betray him. He's the most Milean thing I can think of now. One of the last school-masters in Milea, gone now just like my homestead—but not really. Not while I'm here to draw him, to sing the songs he taught me, to remember like the ungovernable girl I am.

Fee is singing "The Green Fields of Milea." That one was my ma's favorite, and as I hum along and remember her and wish she was here now, words come together in my head. Girls resist. Then they riot. Then they are free. It becomes a half song about everything that's happening here that I wish I could sing to my ma, wherever she is. She's the one who told me to stay free, and I can't bear to fail her twice.

DAY 2 OF
FREE MILEA

I COME INTO THE DINING HALL WITH MY PRIMER
under my arm and spot Fee at a table in the corner, hunched
over something flat and papery. When I pull out a chair next
to her, she looks up abruptly and slides an arm over what
she's doing. That stings—I thought she'd forgiven me, at
least a little—but I pretend not to notice and flip through
the pages of my primer, looking for *C is for Croplands*.

We work in silence, the scritching of lead on paper oddly
comforting, so it's several moments before I realize Fee has
stopped. I risk a glance at her, and she's frowning intently
at her work. I have to keep myself from asking what's
wrong. We're not that kind of friends anymore. We might
never be again.

At length, Fee sits back in her chair and my heart leaps, but she just waves her pencil over her papers and says, "It's too weird. With you sitting here and everything."

"Oh." I toy with a folded-over page corner. "Want me to move?"

Fee shakes her head. "It's just . . . the girls talk about what happened like it's been a song since before the ancestors were born. How the nuns found your plait. How you were shorn, and how you seized the viceroy of New Weald and took him hostage in revenge for leaving you nameless."

A song starts running through my head and takes the shape of the thing she just said, even though that's nowhere near why it happened.

Then I realize the papers Fee is leaning across are covered with stiff but sturdy letters. Wealdan letters, just like the books they made us read.

"I taught myself to write," Fee says, gruff and shy, like I'm going to laugh at her or call her a knuckle-under. "You know how you said I should go to hedge school? We started one. In janitorial."

I struggle for words. Not because of the hedge school. Because Fee writing anything is like Master Grenallan claiming and transforming *ungovernable*.

"I can't write really well or anything," Fee goes on, "but I've been writing down everything that's happened since we took the school. Because honestly? It doesn't feel real. None of it does."

I grin. "No. Not in the slightest."

"I can't make a song about this. I'm no schoolmaster. But there should be some kind of record." Fee gestures around at the dining hall, at girls in their new pink and yellow clothing, eating vegetables and not wearing scarves and not complying to earn privileges. "When the nuns are back, it will all be lost."

"Lost?" I grip my drawing lead. "No way! There might be rules here, but the nuns can't stop us from *talking*. I plan to make friends with each new girl who comes up from lower school and find a way tell her the whole story."

Fee carefully draws another letter. "Jey keeps saying they won't punish everyone, which could be true, but can you really see *no one* getting punished? Who do you think they'll make an example of? And what makes you think any mention of all this won't become an excludable offense? Once the ringleaders have been disappeared, the others will be given one of those choices that isn't a choice—follow them to the workhouse or stay quiet about what we did. Or else."

Master Grenallan told us the Wealdans write everything down and don't bother to memorize anything. Books might be fragile and flammable, but so were the ancestors.

So are we.

"We'll make the emperor include it in our pardon," I tell her. "No punishment for anyone for what they did during the riot. No holding it against us forever, either."

Fee smiles sadly at her papers. "All right. Let's say we really do get a pardon. Let's even say the nuns aren't allowed to retaliate against us and somehow that's enforceable from the provincial capital. It won't matter. Nothing will change. We'll still be stuck at school so we can learn to be useful to the empire. Some of us will be going below again, since unpaid labor is the only way the nuns can afford to run this place. The rest of you?" She makes another letter, slow and careful. "Uniforms. Ranks. Demerits. Informers. Day after day after day, till it's just easier to comply. Because if you believe something like this will ever be permitted to happen again, you are very, very wrong."

"Then we make school better," I say, and then I flinch and add, "What I mean is, I have an idea that could make it better. So we won't have to do something like this again. The ranks and the scarves and the demerits? None of that is in the Education Act. There's no reason for it, other than to get us used to other people deciding who we are and what we're worth. And to remind us what it costs not to comply."

"Oh. Well. In that case, why are you wasting time talking to me?" Fee makes a shooing motion. "Go decide what we should do to be songworthy."

"I'm not deciding anything. Loe wants to do that stuff, so it's probably better if she does. She's not listening, though."

Fee glances at me sidelong. "It's hard to trust someone who wants to be in charge that badly."

I rub my stubbly head. Malliane would know what to say. "You were right. Yesterday, in the nuns' quarters. You were already thinking about *then what?* This is really your idea. I think we should put it to a vote."

"What idea?" Fee asks wearily.

"That we not just negotiate for our lives. There is victory in survival, yes. It can't end there, though. It might be the law that Milean kids have to go to national school, but there's no reason we have to leave it as New Wealdans."

"It won't work," Fee whispers.

I shift my chair closer and wait till she looks up. Her time in janitorial marked her, and not just the faint scalding across her hands and the hollows in her face. There's a terror about her now, something that will make her comply no matter what's asked of her. Not everyone resisted as Milea fell, because not everyone could. That's why the likes of Everard and Jasperine stepped up to resist for everyone.

"Maybe not," I reply, "but that means we lose absolutely nothing by trying."

It takes most of the morning to gather everyone in the dining hall. Almost everyone, that is. I knock on the door of the honor girls' chamber so long my knuckles go raw. Finally Koa opens it the smallest crack, and before I can say a word, she tells me Loe is busy and I'm not to bother her anymore.

"When it's time to tell the nuns whether we'll let the

doctor in to look at the viceroy, Loe will find you," Koa tells me, and as she shuts the door in my face, I hear giggling.

I should tell the honor girls my plan anyway. Shout it through the door. Make Loe angry enough to talk to me. I don't, though. She can go her own way, and so can I.

By noon, the rest of us have a list of demands. We vote. Girls dissent and we talk it over. We vote again and again till it's deep into the afternoon and we have six concessions everyone can agree on. No punishment for any girl for taking part in the protest—no demerits, no correctional vocational training, no workhouse—and we won't be made to put on productions like *The Winning of New Weald*. Parents will be allowed to visit whenever they like, and girls can spend free time with them. No more rules on our appearance; we can wear plain shirts and trousers and bind our hair. Any correctional sentences must have a specific end date that's fair according to the infraction. There won't be any ranks, either. What we eat and what vocational training we do will have nothing to do with how well we comply or inform on someone else.

"If the nuns agree to these concessions—in writing, like something that would hold up in court—we will open the doors." I glance around the room, but no one is standing up to dissent. "We'll let the viceroy be moved to a hospital. We'll go back to class and vocational training. We will behave appropriately and do what we're asked. We'll accept reasonable consequences if we step out of line." I lick my lips. "If the nuns don't agree, we will stay free."

Stay free as long as you can. My ma didn't just mean keep clear of constables who'd enforce the Education Act.

The honor girls are still nowhere in sight, but I'm not going to tell Free Mileans what they should do. Instead I ask Jey to come with me to the roof to deliver the terms just in case the nuns decide to try something dishonest.

I find a place where I don't have to hold on so I can sign for Jey. Sister Gunnhild steps out of a big field tent when I call her name. Her habit is grubby and her veil is on crooked; the nuns must be sleeping rough like graycoats during the Burning Days. Even from this far away, she looks absolutely wrecked.

"How is the viceroy?" Her voice trembles, though she tries to keep it neutral.

"Alive. As well as can be expected. Sedated." I should have gone by the infirmary so I could tell her exactly what his condition is, but as long as he's alive, I really don't care. "Where is the representative from the emperor?"

"On his way. Have you come to make arrangements to let the doctor in to treat the viceroy?"

"We voted against opening the doors for any reason until all our demands are met," I reply.

Sister Gunnhild frowns. "Only the emperor can grant you a pardon, and his emissary is—"

"We have new demands. Simple, reasonable ones." I rub my scruffy head, big and showy. "You're the head nun.

You can grant them easily here and now. Considering how you're going to convince the emperor to give us a pardon, we have every reason to believe we'll be back in school soon with all of this behind us. Right?"

Sister Gunnhild's pleasant, calm expression twitches, but she nods once, curtly.

"We also know you need a pardon as much as we do," I go on, "and we know you wouldn't want anything bad to happen to the viceroy while the emissary is on his way. Would you?"

"What do you want, 1076?"

"I think you mean Malliane Pirine Vinnio Aurelia Hesperus." Even though I have no right to that name, I'm nowhere near 1076 anymore. "I'm just the messenger. These demands come from all of us."

As I recite them, I keep waiting for Sister Gunnhild to turn purple and explode in a fit of rage, but she merely nods along like I'm a novice giving a report. By the time I'm done, Sister Chlotilde has joined her and I'm glad Jey is here, even though I'm a hundred feet up with no way for the nuns to reach me and tear me apart.

"We understand that you girls are upset about the production," Sister Gunnhild replies. "We clearly failed to provide you with enough knowledge of history to appreciate the opportunity we worked so hard to give you. I promise that you will never be asked to perform in another production again."

Jey sits back on her heels. *Holy shrines. Did she agree to one of our demands? Just like that?*

"What about our other demands?" I call down. "I don't think they give special treatment to anyone in the work-house, even nuns."

"School policy was developed by experts to help ensure a successful future for each of you," Sister Gunnhild replies. "The Education Act—"

"Nope, not in the Education Act," I cut in. "Nothing we're asking for is specifically against the law."

Whoa! Jey says. *Sister Chlotilde just cursed out Milean schoolmasters and said the graycoats didn't get to them fast enough.*

"I don't have to justify the Crown's decisions to a cro—" Sister Gunnhild cuts herself off and forces a stiff, polite smile. "Very well. We'll take your requests under advise-ment. You are correct that I do have the authority to make certain changes in my school. I don't want to make prom-ises I can't keep, so I'll need the ledgers from my office to work out what those changes can be. Will you get those to me? Maybe lower them down in a basket on a rope?"

I turn to Jey, relay the nun's request, then ask, *What do you think?*

Are those the big books with the leather bindings? Jey replies. *We may have wrecked them.*

How bad? Can we stuff the pages back between the covers and send them down that way?

Jey squints like she's trying to remember, then nods. *Sister Gunnhild already agreed to one of our demands, and she agreed to it easily. How's it going to look if we refuse to hand over something simple like her books?*

Especially since Sister Gunnhild isn't asking for anything in return, like insisting on us letting in a nun or a novice to make sure the viceroy is even still alive. She's that worried we'll harm him, and that sure at least one of us is capable of it.

"We'll get you the ledgers," I call down, and I hesitate before adding, "Thank you."

Jey and I crawl back toward the maintenance ladder hatch. Halfway there we meet Fee and Nim climbing over the roof toward the edge facing the courtyard. They're each holding the end of a bedsheet, and on it is painted THIS IS FREE MILEA in hulking black letters. They fling the banner over the side of the building and nail the corners to the shingles so it flutters boldly over the front of what used to be Forswelt National School.

The dining hall is silent. Then Mor says, "You can't be serious."

"I sent the ledgers down myself." I'm on a table in the middle of the room where Jey can see me sign and everyone else can hear, and girls have stopped cramming tofu and salad into their mouths to pay attention. "Sister Gunnhild is going to consider our demands."

"All of them?" Gaddy asks pointedly.

I fight a frown. "Sister Gunnhild already agreed never to make us do a production again."

"I'm much more worried about the first demand," Gaddy replies. "The one that says none of us gets punished for any of this."

"We can hold out as long as we need to," I say. "We have enough food and water. They're the ones who have to make concessions. The viceroy still needs proper treatment and the nuns still need a pardon, same as us."

"Something's not right," Nim murmurs. "It's too easy."

Fee is at a table on the edge of the crowd, her packet of papers under her elbow and her pencil working slow but steady.

Girls, Jey says, *we've done something even the flying columns couldn't do. We're about to win. Something tiny, sure. But it's still a win.*

"So that means we need to think about what we do now," I say, glancing at Fee. "School will go back to the way it was if we're not careful. If we don't remember why it was that way in the first place."

Fee looks up.

"The girl on your left? She's your friend. She's as Milean as you. So's the girl on your right. New girls coming up from lower school? Them too. Especially them. Bring them in. We are a flying column and we can stay that way. If we hold this together, we'll always be in Free Milea no matter what it says over the door."

Gaddy starts singing "The Green Fields of Milea" in a clear, pure voice, and before she starts the second verse, I'm on my feet, singing the harmony. We finish the last verse but I keep singing, and it's not "The Green Fields of Milea" anymore but the words that came together in my head about the Forswelt riot, how Free Milean girls refused to comply and made a school their own, how they spoke and sang and did and lived as they chose. How they resisted everything that would have made them enemies of one another, and how every last one was a credit to her ancestors and her name-kin.

When it's done, I sit down. My knees are rubbery. It's one thing to put songs together in my head. Quite another to sing them out like they're the same as the songs that make Mileans who they are.

Nim's hands are flying, trying to make sense of it for Jey. At length she breathes, "That . . . that was a new song. It was a song about us."

How did you make a song? Jey asks.

I hold my hands out to sign, but I don't know what to say. To these girls, I've always been Milean. I'm the one who believed the worst so easily.

Gaddy starts singing my song. Low and tentative, like she's not sure it's allowed. But Emmy picks it up, and Nim, and then girls around the room join one by one—and that's when it hits me.

This is *then what?*

Then what isn't us getting out of this in one piece. It's *how* we're getting out. It's what kind of Mileans we'll be when it's over. We have to get out by holding together. By doing what's best for everyone instead of what's easiest or what's good for one person. By bringing the best parts of the past with us into the future.

The future the Wealdans want me to see is a lodging-house or a servants' quarters, but the one I see is full of girls who I'll keep whispering these things to after lights-out or into the clatter of factory machines. I'll make and remake a primer in every place I find myself. No matter where they send me, no matter what they tell me, I will always sing. I will always be ungovernable. I will always be Milean.

DAY 3 OF FREE MILEA

LOE IS WAITING IN THE CORRIDOR AS I HEAD TO breakfast. "Is it true? Did you really get us amnesty?"

It's hard not to feel smug, but I try to keep it off my face. "I think so. It's not like we're asking them to disband the school and send us home."

"You could have asked for that," Loe replies. "You *should* have. We've got the viceroy. You could have asked for anything."

"*I* didn't ask for anything," I remind her. "*We* decided. All of us together. Besides, what good would a ridiculous demand like that have done? The nuns couldn't send us home even if they wanted to. There's still the Education Act, and that's not going away."

Loe rolls her eyes like I'm a complete fool. Everard Talshine's great-granddaughter clearly feels she has to be songworthy with every breath she draws, as if it's something you can inherit, like straight hair or big feet. Or maybe she figures there's only one way to be songworthy, and it has to be big and showy and fatal. It has to be Jasperine on the pyre, the Hanged Maidens on their gallows, Everard torn to pieces.

If we are all schoolmasters now, there are as many ways to be songworthy as there are to be Milean.

"Want to come up to the roof with me and Jey?" I ask. "I'm going to see if the emissary has come yet."

Loe raises a suspicious eyebrow. "Really? Me?"

"We're surrounded outside by very scared nuns, and in here by girls who are looking to us to keep them safe," I reply softly. "Who does it help if you and I aren't friends?"

She squints at nothing for a long moment, then says, "I'm still angry about what you did."

"I know." We don't all come to this equally. It's going to take Loe longer to open her hand. "But I hope you're angrier about what the Wealdans are doing to all of us."

Loe sighs and falls into step at my elbow. It would be easy to rub it in a little, to notice aloud oh-so-sweetly how many times just today I've been given that flying-column commander salute, but even though Loe has not always been nice to me, she is not my enemy.

We meet Jey outside the dining hall, and together the three of us climb the ladders one after another, but even halfway across the roof I know something's not right. I stop short, a cold breeze scritching my tufty head, and that's when I hear the tinkle-champ of metal and leather that only means one thing.

Graycoats.

The courtyard is crawling with them. Hundreds of them. Maybe a whole regiment. Graycoats and horses and a military-grade battering ram and it's the Sutherland Fair and my da can't keep hold of my slippery little hand and I'm wailing and one of the butchers backhands me across the face and hollers *shut up* and I don't, I can't, and I blink it away because if graycoats have been called to Forswelt, they're here to storm the building.

Standing front and center of the squad is Captain Lennart, a commander's plume in his hat, frowning thoughtfully at the front door. The last time I saw him, he chased me across Trelawney Crossing at the head of a constabulary force. The time before that, he escorted my parents out of the courtroom and through surging crowds of Wealdans holding up nooses and shouting for a return to the hanging tree, all the way to the detention center.

But Captain Lennart is not a constable anymore. He's passed the military exam. He's a graycoat now.

Captain Lennart spots us and gestures to an officer, who steps forward and uncurls a piece of paper. "In accordance with the will of our most sovereign emperor, let it be known . . ."

He keeps reading, but I already know every word of the Assembly Restriction Act because Master Grenallan did what he could to prepare us, and not just for national school. Now that they've read it aloud, they're within their legal right to do whatever it takes to break up what they've decided is an illegal gathering, and this time my da's not here to save me.

"Sister Gunnhild never sent for someone from the imperial court." Loe is barely breathing as she takes in the hulking soldiers in our courtyard with their rifles and bayonets and their massive, sturdy long knives that can rip someone open from neck to belly button in a single slice. "That stupid nun sent for these butchers instead."

She stalled us, too. She strung us along to give them time to arrive. Asking for her ledgers with the right mix of foot-dragging and worry and grudging compliance so we'd think we were winning.

Our families will get the bill for this. Calling out the graycoats. Jey looks bellysick. *The Crown will make them pay back what it cost to put down our rebellion. Like the grands had to work off the price of the invasion of Milea.*

That means indenture. No one's family has any money. It all goes to tithes to the church and dues to the landlord, so to pay back this debt, my friends' parents will have to bind themselves to a factory owner and work till they die, because like demerits below, those debts never seem to get paid no matter how much work you do.

My ma and da were caught in a granary. They'd rigged it to blow up and take them with it alongside any soldiers who tried to capture them, but the bomb squad got there first and cut the connections and my ma snicked the ignition wires together and nothing happened and that's the way the graycoats took them into custody, each bellowing "Everard's Flying Column" as they were kicked and wrestled into a detention wagon.

"Present the ringleader," Captain Lennart calls up. I want to say I hear an echo of the sympathy he once had for a wide-eyed, tear-streaked girl who clung to her da's manacled hand in the courtroom for more moments than the captain of the constabulary should have allowed.

There's a lot of things I want right now.

I have enough songs to know *present the ringleader* is a lot like *face the room,* so I shout down, "Jasperine Vesley is in charge of this school. We are her representatives. We want—"

"The Crown has declared a state of insurrection, and under the provisions of the Loyalty Act, all persons associated with this insurrection are to be treated as enemy combatants and traitors to the empire, which means Crown forces have a standing order to shoot to kill."

Songs start running through my head. "Shoot to Kill," version after version, which tells how the Lost Generation was sent into tenant crofts and factories for a handful of copper coins, after the passing of the Forest Acts made sure a living couldn't be had any other way. The Crown doesn't martyr Mileans anymore, but today they're going to. By sundown, every last girl in this building will be dead.

"However, the Crown recognizes the youth of the rebels and the congenital ignorance of New Wealdans as a people," Captain Lennart goes on, "and it is reluctant to shed the blood of foolish but otherwise useful subjects who have been misled and coerced and intimidated by malcontents into this act of defiance. To that end, the Crown is prepared to accept the unconditional surrender of this building in exchange for mercy. If the doors are unlocked and the nuns readmitted before midday today, students who had no active part in the insurrection will be relocated to other national schools around New Weald to continue their education. The ringleaders will be publicly shorn and branded with the Embattled Crown, then sent immediately into factory service."

I cackle and run a hand over my tufty head. It's nothing worse than what's already happened to me, or will eventually happen once I *graduate* from this excuse for a school. As for the branding—nothing will ever hurt as much as losing my name-kin to the shears. But Loe pulls in a series of harsh, terrified breaths and rubs her haunch like someone who's seen the irons in action. All I've seen is the aftermath, that night in the guardhouse with my parents barely moving and the stink of cooked flesh damp like a fog, and I can't help but shudder.

"They will also publicly take the loyalty oath to the emperor," Captain Lennart adds, "in his majestic presence."

"No," Loe whispers. "No way. Not happening. None of my ancestors ever knelt before any of his. I'm not going to be the one who starts."

"If the doors are not unlocked by midday, Crown soldiers will retake the building by force. Students who took no active part in this insurrection will still be relocated, but their files will be marked and they will never be permitted to rise above fourth rank. The ringleaders will be broken in the workhouse."

Captain Lennart turns on his heel, proper and military, and disappears into a tent. There's no sign of nuns anywhere, just an endless swath of graycoats who will have no interest in negotiating and may not have heard anything too clearly after *shoot to kill* came out of their commander's mouth.

Jey and Loe and I make it off the roof. We find ourselves at the bottom of the maintenance ladder. I'm going to be sick. It's all I can do to translate what just happened for Jey, who's clearly fighting panic. Somehow I believed the nuns really meant to negotiate. Somehow I thought this could have ended with school even the smallest bit better. Jey is corpse-pale, her hands unusually still, but Loe has gone steely.

"We hold. That door is sturdy. We've got enough water. Let them *try* to take this school by force." Loe is pacing, muttering. "We'll pick up kitchen knives and garden trowels like girls did during the Burning Days."

Outside are the men who broke the flying columns. Who burned the boats they came in so there'd be no turning back. They'll get through that door. They'll come in shooting. This has gone too far for them to leave any of us alive. They can't send anyone to other schools. If even the smallest whisper of what we did survives us, the national school movement will never recover and reform will be impossible.

The Crown will learn from this, like they learned not to martyr the likes of Jasperine and Everard. They'll tighten the ranks. They'll turn every last girl into an informer. They'll never, *never* make the mistake of allowing something like a production to show us how we can work together in a common cause against our common enemy. An enemy that is not other Mileans, but those who would set us against one another.

"I'm not taking that oath." Loe is still growling, fierce and oblivious. "I cannot and *will not* face my great-grandda in the afterlife with that hanging around my neck. We're not surrendering and that's final."

Holding out would be songworthy. So very songworthy. It'll also be costly, and there's a difference between ungovernable and unwise. I swallow hard and put myself in Loe's path. "Nothing's final till we vote. This is Free Milea, and we follow the vote."

"Everard Talshine did not die horribly for me to surrender when I could die for Milea and join him on the Roll of Honor!"

"Loe?" I say quietly. "We're already on the Roll of Honor. You. Me. Everyone here."

"You can't just—"

"We seized a school. We took the viceroy of New Weald hostage. We've been free for three days. That's more than even the flying columns managed."

There's a muffled crack and the walls shudder. Tiny puffs of dust and grit come raining down between the wall stones.

Jey's eyes go huge. *What was that?*

At the Sutherland Fair they didn't wait for the fairgoers to comply. I turn slow and shaky to Jey and Loe. "They're not going to give us till midday. They're coming in now."

The stone around the big front door is webbed with cracks, and there's a screely metal-on-metal sound that's got to be a graycoat working on the hinges with a crowbar. The whole corridor smells scorched and there's a faint curl of smoke along the floor.

Jey sees me frowning in confusion and says, *Black powder. Stinks, right? They must want to weaken the door before they try the ram. That, and make sure we're terrified.*

"Go tell everyone to hole up in their chambers," I say to Loe. "They'll have half a chance then."

"No way," Loe replies, but she says it to the front door and the big locks that are beginning to shudder from the force of the crowbar on the other side. "When they come in shooting, I'm going to be right here. I'm not going to the workhouse and I'm not taking any oath. I'm an enemy combatant and I'm going to make them put me straight onto the Roll of Honor the proper way."

Jey glances uneasily at the door. *I'll go. Just in case it matters.*

A sharp whiff of black powder, then *crack!* This time the door shudders and dances on its hinges.

It's not going to take many more blasts.

My primer. I paw at my hip, but I didn't grab my carry-bag on my way out of my chamber this morning. They'll find my primer and destroy it. But not before they learn from it. They'll start locking up the books and the nuns will check them every day so no other girl will ever know it's possible to be ungovernable. I won't be here to pull her into a hedge school like Emmy did for me. There won't be anything to tell her that it's possible to make it out of here a Milean.

So she won't. None of them will.

The nuns will be more careful with the girls who come after us. Those girls will never know what happened when we resisted together instead of caring only about ourselves. That story will be disappeared with us and buried for good, just like Fee said.

My ma and da didn't leave me out of the machine breaking because they thought I wasn't songworthy. They left me out so there'd be someone to remember what they did and why they did it. Someone to remember they were ever here.

I fly down the corridor, dodging girls who are carrying chairs and tables from the dining hall. They're heading toward the front door, and it's only when I'm well past them that I realize they're not hiding in their rooms like they should be if they don't want to get shot. They're putting up barricades. They're going to fight.

In the doorway of my chamber I crash hard into Nim coming out. Both of us stumble back, so it takes me a moment to notice she's holding my carrybag in both hands. No. She's hugging it against her chest like it's precious. Like she knows exactly what it is and what will soon happen to it.

"It was you," I breathe. "You're her."

Nim blinks back tears as she nods.

"And you made the first one, too. Are you . . . Jasperine's great-granddaughter?"

Nim laughs aloud, harsh. "I'm not anything. Definitely not any part of Jasperine. But that story sounds better, doesn't it? Like something out of a song."

Once upon a time I thought only someone like Loe and her ancestor on the Roll of Honor would ever be able to make something like the primer.

"Not anything?" I repeat. "No. No one gets to tell you

that. Not Wealdans. Not Mileans. You are here—" I want to use her Milean name, but her simple three-strand braids tell me nothing and I can only manage, "You are here, alive, when honestly none of us should be. That's what makes you someone, and only you get to decide who that is."

Nim studies the floor, and it's quiet for a long moment before she holds up the bag. "By the way? You can't draw. You're terrible at it." I snuffle a laugh, and she adds, "I just . . . I can't lose another book. Like that last one."

She must have heard how some stupid girl held on to the primer too hard and lost it for everyone. Or maybe she looked for it. She sneaked into Sister Chlotilde's classroom just to flip the pages and it wasn't there.

"This one's going somewhere safe," I choke-whisper. "Come with me."

Nim shoves the carrybag at me. "I can't watch. Sorry. I just can't." And she's off down the corridor, her bright topknot a curl of brassy color. Nim, who has more Roll of Honor guts than I'll ever have to face this nameless.

I find Fee sitting in a corner of the dining hall, her papers on the floor, writing in hurried, messy strokes. When I kneel beside her, she looks up, terrified. "Jey said the graycoats are coming for us. My story's not finished. There's so much I missed."

"It's ours, though. Made by us, about us. That's why we've got to bury it. Whatever you've written."

"No!" Fee covers her papers protectively. "Do you have

any idea how long it took me to write this much? It'll be lost forever!"

"So being caught with it will keep it safe somehow?" I show her the primer, turning the pages one by one—Fee stares in disbelief—then I rip them out of their pasteboard binding and fold them into a tight packet. "We'll wrap these pages in oilpaper, yours and mine, and bury them out by the pump where there's dirt, and maybe one day a girl will find them. She'll know we were here. She'll know what we did, even if we're not here to tell her. That's how we'll win. That's how we'll survive."

"Just let me finish this part." A teardrop splashes, wrinkling a circle into the page. Fee blots it, then traces over the smudgy letters so the word is clear: *together.*

In a quiet corner of the pump yard, I dig a hole while Fee solemnly wraps our pages in a sheet of waxy paper we found covering a cheese. When the hole is deep enough, Fee carefully arranges the packet at the bottom like we're burying a pet or a baby sister. We both kneel and smooth the dirt clean and undisturbed. Malliane may have forgotten me, but I press my scarred hands against the ground where the history of Free Milea is buried and I beg her to see this one last thing. What happens next is going to be costly, but some part of it can survive us, and though no one will ever sing of our deeds, maybe one day someone will know the girls of Free Milea were here.

I leave Fee kneeling by the pump and hurry through

the dining hall. The entire corridor between it and the front door has been rigged with barricades. Throughout the hallway, girls are singing my song in Milean—my new song, about us, in one big grand offense. Jey appears at my elbow, but she can't sign because she's holding something. It looks like a furry pet, maybe a rabbit, but then I realize it's made of plaits. It's made of Malliane's plaits, and as Jey puts it into my hands, it becomes a false topknot.

Jey halfway smiles, shows me a tuft of hair against her neck, then points to the hairpiece in my hands. Sure enough, there's Jey's auburn hair, carefully braided into Malliane's plait and wound into a topknot along with dozens in other colors and textures.

My breath catches.

Every girl in this room must have given a braid. She must have unplaited one of her own, reworked it into Malliane's pattern, then brought metal against her hair and cut. These girls were never asleep. They were resisting in their own way. All I did was let them go those ways, and now here we are, all together.

I settle the hairpiece on my head. There's a grippy substance on the underside that grabs my stubbly scalp, and the girls start clapping and cheering, even now, even when we're all about to meet our ancestors.

Malliane never turned her back on me after all. Somehow she knew me. Somehow she always will.

I hug Jey fierce and sure, and then we head through

the barricade warren to the very first one, where I know I'll find Loe. The walls shudder again, and there's a sturdy crack and graycoats' voices growling approval at the quality of the explosives. The first barricade is made of two dining-hall tables shoved together and reinforced with Sister Gunnhild's big desk. Loe shifts enough to make room for me to climb on. Nim is with her, and Jey and I scrabble up alongside them.

This is nowhere near what it feels like to die by fire. This is what it feels like to die standing, to carry your crowbar and kerosene into machine sheds, to decide there's only so far you'll go to comply. Next to me, Nim is whispering the Roll of Honor. She's taken her hair out of those three-strand braids and replaited them into Malliane's pattern. We're name-kin now. She's chosen Malliane as surely as Malliane has chosen me. Nim has brought something of the past into her present, and what's left of her future.

A hatchet against wood, splintery and choppy. The graycoats will break through any moment now. There's no shame in being captured. Jasperine was. Everard, too, and Hesperus and Aurelia and men and women and girls like me who I know a thousand songs about.

There won't be any songs about me.

There's a massive echo as the door is blown off its hinges and hits the floor stones. I suck in a sharp breath and brace hard, but there's no hail of bullets. No trampling graycoat onslaught and flashing bayonet charge. There's a *tinkle-tink* of metal hitting the floor, then a sharp, loud hissing as the corridor fills with smoke.

"Girls of Forswelt!" a man's voice calls. "This school is now under the authority of the emperor. Line up against the walls with your hands in plain sight. The ringleaders of this incident have been identified and will be taken into custody and immediately sent to the workhouse."

"No." Loe covers her mouth with her sleeve. "They said shoot to kill. They have to martyr us!"

On my other side, Nim is coughing and choking and gagging. My eyes water and my throat is on fire and something hits my shoulder and I stumble and fall off Sister Gunnhild's desk and jam my elbow so badly I screech. My hairpiece slides off my head and I grapple for it, one-handed, rasping for a single breath in the dim corridor. Someone wearing glass goggles and a rubber mask hauls me up. It's Captain Lennart, and he peers into my face, then dodges the knuckles I haphazardly aim at his chin. Even behind the goggles I see the flicker of recognition and then another of sympathy.

"Got one," Captain Lennart says over his shoulder. "Careful. I don't think the gas is strong enough."

"Kill me," Loe snarls, but the graycoat merely pins her arms behind her back and shoulders her toward the door.

Another graycoat is trying to move the table and get past, but Jey has wedged a chair under it, and she and Koa are standing arm in arm so he can't just shove it away. The soldiers have clearly been given orders not to harm us.

That means they don't really consider us enemy combatants. We're just girls. Ignorant, misguided girls who were too frightened to ignore troublemakers and malcontents, who will readily comply and fade back into the national school system if the consequences otherwise are fearful enough.

The singing is growing louder, especially from the end of the corridor that the gas has not yet reached. More metal cans go *tinkle-hiss* in the chaos. Graycoats strong-arm their way toward the dining hall, cursing as they find barricades and ungovernable girls who won't line up against the wall and show their hands, even though they're doubled over coughing and kicking at shins and scrubbing at their streaming eyes. These are graycoats who have never seen Free Mileans.

My field captains have both been taken. Nim and Jey each stand bound and terrified in front of a graycoat. Loe and Koa, too, and one by one they're being marched out the broken hole that once was the front door. They chose this. We all did, but that makes it no easier to watch a reddening patch over Jey's eye grow steadily darker or Nim's head jerk as a narrow plait disappears from her topknot into a dingy coat pocket.

Maybe this is why my parents really kept me out of the field rebellion. They knew they would fold in an instant if someone they loved beyond reason was hurt to force their compliance.

The singing echoes down the corridor now, eerie and disembodied from the lingering smoke. It's still my song, and this will have to be enough. Maybe one of these girls, wherever she's sent, will be shoveling manure with the rest of the orange scarves and a fragment of this song will slip through her mind and she'll remember that one time she spent three days free.

Captain Lennart is threading a thick strand of rope over my wrists, muttering how it's a bloody shame. His lieutenant calls through the doorway that the detention wagon is ready. Behind me, the barricades are falling one by one as graycoats with cudgels and big bare hands kick and batter and throw pieces aside, and smoke-smudged girls are being pulled out from the rubble of smashed desk legs and tabletops and manhandled into a line against the wall.

No one is complying, though. No one is flinging a hand up to inform. They are singing louder, even as their wrists are being bound or they're slapped across the mouth, even as they're choking and coughing out the words. Three days ago we were New Wealdans. Today we are Free Mileans, all of us together.

That's further than I thought any of us could come.

The song changes, and the girls sing a new verse I didn't make, and it's about Malley's flying column and how we held the school for three days and spent every one of them free because I told them they could.

My name is being sung.

Something of this will survive me.

We are all schoolmasters now.

The graycoats securing my field captains escort them from the building, one after another. I'm next, and Captain Lennart hauls me toward a detention wagon that looks very familiar from all those weeks and months ago.

Only it's not. Jey and Nim are seated there already. Loe and Koa sit tall and defiant on the opposite bench. We'll be different from the other workhouse inmates. None of us is alone. We are more than ungovernable now. We have been free.

Because they can send us to the workhouse. Whether they can break us there is another matter.

ACKNOWLEDGMENTS

MANY THANKS TO:

Katherine Longshore, for improving this book considerably with feedback, encouragement, and friendship.

Jenna Beacom, for providing valuable commentary on the representation of deafness and the Deaf community. Any remaining inaccuracies or inadequacies are mine alone.

Ammi-Joan Paquette, my supportive, hard-working agent.

Reka Simonsen, my wonderful, insightful editor.

The team at Atheneum for all their effort behind the scenes.

Readers everywhere, and anyone who puts books into kids' hands.

A Reading Group Guide to

R Is for Rebel

by J. Anderson Coats

Discussion Questions

1. What is national school, and why does Malley have to attend? In our world, education is almost always viewed as a positive thing. Why do you think Malley doesn't want to go?

2. Why do you think the emperor has implemented the Education Act that requires all Milean children to attend national schools? Why can't kids live at home and go to school during the day?

3. Consider how standardized forms of schooling act as a form of social control. What do children learn in school, and who does it benefit? Historically, do you think children from all backgrounds experienced public education the same way? What are some similarities and differences? What are some reasons these differences might exist? What has changed over time, and what remains the same?

4. What happens to Malley after she arrives at school? What is asked of her? Why does she object? Why do you think the schools are structured the way they are?

5. Why do you think Milean children aren't allowed to braid and bind their hair at school? Malley's hair is central to who she is. What do you hold on to as part of your identity? What would happen if that was taken away—how would you feel, and what would you want to do next?

6. One of Malley's first acts of resistance is to sing a song about an event in Milean history. What is this event, and what can you infer about the relationship between Milea and Weald? What can you infer about Milean culture from Malley's action?

7. What is the Roll of Honor? What purpose does it have in Milean society? How does this relate to the Wealdans' list of "prohibited names"?

8. Why are students given a new name when they enroll in school? What message does it send if someone's name is a regular word instead of a proper name? For whom is this message intended?

9. What do you think about Sister Chlotilde's assertion that the play the girls are to put on is "historically accurate"?

What makes something historically accurate? How can stories be used to persuade and influence people's thinking, as well as entertain?

10. How do the Milean girls understand the events of the play? What is included, what is left out, and how have details been framed to emphasize a particular story? How have the Wealdans interpreted these events, and why?

11. Why does Malley take the blame for the seditious primer? Do you agree with her decision? Do you think Sister Chlotilde would believe her if she said she didn't ruin the book?

12. Discuss the purpose of the songs in Milean society. When Malley says she wants to be songworthy, what does she mean? What does it tell us about identity? About history?

13. What are the strengths and drawbacks of maintaining a record of the past in a purely verbal way? What are the strengths and weaknesses of a written record?

14. Why is Malley's time in the laundry important? What does she learn there?

15. Malley realizes she's in the laundry because she resisted, but she is convinced she's the only person who's doing so.

Do the other girls agree? Do you? Identify instances in the story where other students resist in ways that may not be obvious.

16. What mechanisms of control do the Wealdans use to keep the girls in line? How does peer monitoring and the demerit system complicate Malley's desire to resist? Do you think it's better than the government using violence to keep control, or worse?

17. Describe what happens over the course of the rehearsals leading up to the production. How are the girls different? What has changed? Why do they finally decide to take action?

18. What is Free Milea? What do the girls do there? What can we infer about Milean culture from these things? What can we infer about how successfully the school is conditioning the girls into accepting Wealdan ways of doing things?

19. At the beginning of the story, Malley had a specific understanding of leadership. How and why have her views changed by the end?

20. How do you think Wealdan history books will describe what happened at the school? Do you think it will be included in a Wealdan history book at all?

21. Do any aspects of this invented world remind you of our own?

22. Discuss the beliefs and actions of groups in our society today that feel that their culture is being threatened. How are they responding? Compare and contrast the tactics currently being used to preserve those cultures and/or belief systems against the tactics employed in *R Is for Rebel*.

23. At the end of the story, the girls don't seem to "win." They don't get concessions to make school better and they don't cause the Education Act to be repealed. What do you think happens to Malley and the other ringleaders after they arrive at the workhouse? What about the girls who sang?

Turn the page for a sneak peek at
The Many Reflections of Miss Jane Deming.

MRS. D SAID TO LEAVE THE PACKING TO HER, BUT when she wasn't looking, I pulled out a half-size carpetbag I made from a flour sack and put in the things I don't trust her with.

My lucky hopscotch stone.

Three hairpins I found in the big girls' yard behind the schoolhouse from back when I went to school.

The little book Miss Bradley made for me from folded sheets of cheap blank ragpaper that she stitched up the spine with packing cord.

We've been staying at Lovejoy's Hotel in New York City for two days before I get careless and go through my secret carpetbag when Mrs. D is only halfway out the door.

In three steps she's standing over me, holding out her hand. "I must have that paper, Jane."

"Why?" I ask, and it's a perfectly reasonable question, but her brows twitch and her mouth goes tight and straight.

Usually when Mrs. D makes that face, it's followed by her telling me how easy it would be for her to entrust my growing-up years to a Mother who keeps one of the mill-run boardinghouses back in Lowell. Those mills are desperate for girls to stand behind the looms now that the war is over.

Instead, she sighs like I'm simple. "In case I need to write to Mr. Mercer about the voyage. Now, do as you're told."

Mrs. D hasn't exactly *told* me to do anything, and it's not like she can write real good anyway.

"The pages are all filled up," I reply, and I show her the ones at the front that are covered with copy exercises and sums.

She narrows her eyes but lets me keep it.

There are exactly seven blank pages at the end, but there's no reason Mrs. D has to know that. It won't be long before this little book will be useful once more.

We're a week at Lovejoy's before another member of Mr. Mercer's expedition arrives. She's called Miss Gower, and she barely gets through her nice-to-meet-yous before she tells us she already wrote to Washington's territorial governor to ask that she be officially recognized as the Old Maid of the Territory.

There's a pained silence. Being an old maid is akin to having a dire sickness or expecting a baby—something you don't mention in polite company. Mrs. D looks faintly disgusted, like she's about to change a very full diaper, but I blurt, "What did he say?"

"Hsst!" Mrs. D gives me a Look. "Children should be seen and—"

"He agreed, of course." There's more than a hint of pride in Miss Gower's voice and half a chortle. "It's best to call things as they are, and an old maid is definitely what I am and will remain, come what may. What should I call you?"

"Who? Me?"

Miss Gower nods. She's not even looking at Mrs. D.

"J-Jane." I stand a little straighter, like I'm back at school giving a recitation. "Ma'am."

"My stepdaughter," Mrs. D adds with a sigh, "who really ought to know better than to speak to her elders in such a way."

Whenever Mrs. D says things like this, I try not to giggle or roll my eyes. She's only two and twenty, and she doesn't look old enough to say things like *Children should be seen and not heard*.

She means them, though.

"This little charmer is my son, Jeremiah. We call him Jer." Mrs. D turns Jer toward Miss Gower, since this is usually the part where grown-ups coo and make a sappy face to get him to smile.

Miss Gower's brows twitch. "I so dislike the prefix *step*. It implies partitions in a family that holy wedlock should render obsolete."

Papa said almost the same thing on their wedding day. *We're all Demings now. Steps are for walking down.*

"Hmm. Well." Mrs. D smiles all tight-lipped and pointy. "Do pardon us. The baby needs his rest. Jane?"

"Yes, ma'am." As I close the door, Miss Gower is shaking her head like she just saw something impossible or ridiculous or both.

I like to think Papa would do something akin to that if he were still alive. That he'd notice Mrs. D sighing over my sawdusty bread and dirty fingernails and ask her to help me mix better or scrub harder instead of complain. He'd have surely given back all the dolls and skipping ropes and other *childish things* she made me hand over the day she had Jer. I like to think he'd be taking my side.

☙ ☙ ☙

Mr. Mercer comes by the hotel again today to assure us we'll be under way anytime now, bound for Washington Territory, where there are limitless opportunities for individuals of excellent character and the climate is positively Mediterranean. A number of us in his expedition are staying at Lovejoy's, waiting for him to complete the arrangements.

The steamship was supposed to sail back in September. January's half over, and we've heard *anytime now* since Christmas. No one wants to say what at least some of us are thinking: Perhaps Mr. Mercer is a confidence man who has pocketed our passage money and plans to run off with it.

If that were true, though, he'd surely be long gone by now. No, he's probably trying to find just the right ship. It will need to be grand if it's to fit the seven hundred unmarried girls and war widows Mr. Mercer plans to bring out west to teach in the schools of Washington Territory or to turn their hands to other useful employment.

Or, if you are Mrs. D, marry one of the many prosperous gentlemen bachelors pining for quality female society.

She's pinned all her hopes on it. Mrs. D hated working in the Lowell mills. She hated leaving her kitchen and hearth and standing for fourteen hours a day before a loom, sneezing from all the dust and lint and not being able to sleep at night because of the ringing in her ears. She wants to be a wife again, to have someone else go out to work while she keeps house. If she has to go all the way to Washington Territory to do it, by golly, that's what she'll do.

After Mrs. D paid our passage, Mr. Mercer gave her a copy of a pamphlet he wrote about the advantages and charms of Washington Territory. She glanced at it once, rolled her eyes, then left it on her chair in the dining room. I snatched it up and hid it in my secret carpetbag, and when she's not around, I read it.

I've read every word hundreds of times. Even the big words I must puzzle over. Even the boring chapters on Lumber and Trade.

My favorite part is the last chapter, Reflections Upon the Foregoing, where Mr. Mercer writes about the sort of person who would want to go to Washington Territory. An unspoiled and majestic place, he says, a place ideally suited to men of broad mind and sturdy constitution who seek to make a home through industry and wit.

The same must be true for girls of broad mind and sturdy constitution. Otherwise Mr. Mercer would never think to bring us out there. My constitution is sturdy enough. After Jer was born, I got strong hauling buckets of water and scrubbing diaper after diaper on a secondhand washboard.

The problem is my mind. It might not be suitably broad.

When Jer was just weeks old, I had to stay home from school to look after him while Mrs. D went out to work. I never much cared for school till I had something to compare it to. Suddenly all the braid-pulling boys and backside-bruising seats and longhand division and terrifying recitations in front of a frowning Miss Bradley weren't so bad after all. Not when you put it against the endless trudge of keeping house, where there's always one more thing to clean. Not when strangers on the street call you *poor dear* and cluck and sigh over all the fatherless children.

Beatrice was the first of my friends who stopped coming around. Jer cried the whole visit, and I couldn't even offer tea because the fire kept going out. Not that there was anything to talk about. I didn't know the new girl at school, and Beatrice didn't care how hard it was to dry diapers when the weather was damp.

Elizabeth and Violet didn't make it past the threshold.

It could have been different. It *should* have been different. Papa and Mrs. D were married when the war was going to be over by Christmas. Of 1861.

In Washington Territory they probably barely even knew there *was* a war. Just stepping off the boat in a place like that will give all of us what we want. Mrs. D will have her hearth. Jer will have his mama. Since she's set on remarrying, better it be to a man who made his way west before any shots were fired on Fort Anywhere. A man with all his limbs, who doesn't cringe when there's a sudden loud noise. He'll step right out of the chapter on Trade, maybe, or Civil Government, tall and handsome and happy to give Mrs. D whatever she wants, so she'll smile at me and mean it, then tell me to run along and play and be home in time for supper.

I will have ordinary chores and lots of friends. I will have a dress that fits. I'll spend my days in a schoolhouse instead of being someone's *little mother*, as the mill girls would say. I will have limitless opportunities because of my sturdy constitution and a mind I hope to broaden. No one will ever call me *poor dear*.

No one will ever have cause to.

It's been sleeting all morning, so Jer and I can't play outside. Jer just turned two and already he's trying to talk. Ever since we got to New York, the only thing he wants to talk about is carriages.

"Daney! Tarij. Tarij Daney *yes!*" Jer bounces on the bed in our room and points out the window at the sliver of street crowded with people and horses and wagons.

"You might *think* you want to sit out front and watch

carriages," I tell him, "but it's too cold, so what you *really* want is to hear me reread Reflections Upon the Foregoing."

"Tarij," he repeats stubbornly, so I shrug and leave him at the window and read aloud anyway.

My brother doesn't need to hear Mr. Mercer's reflections the way I do. Saying the words out loud makes Washington Territory feel like a secret that's been kept just for me, and it's going to change everything.